I0656925

William Hayley

The Plays and Poems by William Hayley

Vol. V

William Hayley

The Plays and Poems by William Hayley
Vol. V

ISBN/EAN: 9783744710077

Printed in Europe, USA, Canada, Australia, Japan

Cover: Foto ©Andreas Hilbeck / pixelio.de

More available books at **www.hansebooks.com**

P O E M S

A N D

P L A Y S,

By WILLIAM HAYLEY, Esq.

IN SIX VOLUMES.

A NEW EDITION.

VOL. V.

L O N D O N:

PRINTED FOR T. CADELL, IN THE STRAND.

M.DCC.LXXXVIII.

THE

TRIUMPHS OF TEMPER;

A

P O E M:

IN SIX CANTOS.

O VOI CH' AVETE GL' INTELLETTI SANI
MIRATE LA DOTTRINA, CHE SI ASCONDE
SOTTO' IL VELAME DEGLI VERSI STRANI.

DANTE, Inferno, Canto 9.

VOL. V.   B

PREFACE.

IT seems to be a kind of duty incumbent on those who devote themselves to Poetry, to raise, if possible, the dignity of a declining Art, by making it as beneficial to Life and Manners as the limits of Composition, and the character of modern Times, will allow. The ages, indeed, are past, in which the song of the Poet was idolized for its miraculous effects ; yet a Poem, intended to promote the cultivation of good-humour, may still perhaps be fortunate enough to prove of some little service to society in general; or, if this idea may be thought too chimerical and romantic by sober Reason, it is at least one of those pleasing and innocent delusions, in which a poetical Enthusiast may be safely indulged.

The following production owes its existence to an incident in real life, very similar to the principal action of

the

the last Canto; but in forming the general plan of the work, it seemed to me absolutely necessary to introduce both the agency and the abode of *SPLEEN*, notwithstanding the difficulty and the hazard of attempting a subject so happily executed by the masterly pencil of Pope. I considered his Cave of Spleen as a most exquisite cabinet picture; and, to avoid the servility of imitation, I determined to sketch the mansion of this gloomy Power on a much wider canvas: Happy, indeed, if the judgment of the Public may enable me to exclaim, with the honest vanity of the Painter, who compared his own works to the divine productions of Raphael,

" E son Pittore anch' Io!"

The celebrated *Alessandro Tassoni*, who is generally considered as the inventor of the modern Heroi-comic Poetry, was so proud of having extended the limits of his art by a new kind of composition, that he not only spoke of it with infinite exultation in one of his private letters, but even gave a *MS.* copy of his work to his native city of *Modena*, with an inscription, in which he stiled it a new species of Poetry, invented by himself.

A few

A few partial friends have asserted, that the present performance has some degree of similar merit; but as I apprehend all the novelty it possesses, may rather require an apology, than entitle its Author to challenge commendation, I shall explain how far the conduct of the Poem differs from the most approved models in this mode of writing, and slightly mention the poetical effects, which such a variation appeared likely to produce.

It is well known, that the favourite Poems, which blend the serious and the comic, represent their principal characters in a satirical point of view: It was the intention of Tassoni (though prudence made him attempt to conceal it) to satirize a particular Italian Nobleman, who happened to be the object of his resentment. Boileau openly ridicules the French Ecclesiastics in his Lutrin; Garth, our English Physicians, in his Dispensary; and the Rape of the Lock itself, that most excellent and enchanting Poem, which I never contemplate but with new idolatry, is denominated the best Satire extant, by the learned Dr. Warton, in his very elegant and ingenious, but severe, Essay on Pope: A sentence which seems to be confirmed by the Poet himself, in his letter to Mrs. Fermor, where he says, "the cha-

"ra舳er

" racter of *Belinda*, as it is now managed, resembles
" you in nothing but in beauty." Though I think, that
no composition can surpass, or perhaps ever equal this
most happy effort of Genius, as a sportive Satire, I ima-
gined it might be possible to give a new *Character* to this
mixed species of Poetry, and to render it by its *Object*,
though not in its Execution, more noble than the most
beautiful and refined Satire can be. We have seen it
carried to inimitable perfection, in the most delicate
raillery on Female Foibles :—It remained to be tried, if
it might not also aspire to delineate the more engaging
features of Female Excellence.   The idea appeared to
me worth the experiment; for, if it succeeded, it seemed
to promise a double advantage ; first, it would give an
air of novelty to the Poem ; and, secondly, what I
thought of much greater importance, it would render it
more interesting to the heart.   On these principles, I
have endeavoured to paint SERENA as a most lovely, engaging, and accomplished character ; yet I hope the co-
louring is so faithfully copied from general Nature,
that every man, who reads the Poem, may be happy
enough to know many Fair ones, who resemble my
~~Heroine.~~

There

There is another point, in which I have also at-
tempted to give this Poem an air of novelty : I mean,
the manner of connecting the real and the visionary
scenes, which compose it ; by shifting these in alternate
Cantos, I hoped to make familiar Incident and allego-
rical Picture afford a strong relief to each other, and
keep the attention of the Reader alive, by an appear-
ance particularly diversified. I wished, indeed (but I
fear most ineffectually) for powers to unite some touches
of the sportive wildness of Ariosto, and the more seri-
ous sublime painting of Dante, with some portion of the
enchanting elegance, the refined imagination, and the
moral graces of Pope ; and to do this, if possible, with-
out violating those rules of propriety, which Mr. Cam-
bridge has illustrated, by example as well as precept, in
the Scribleriad, and in his sensible Preface to that ele-
gant and learned Poem.

I have now very frankly informed my Reader of the
extent, or rather the extravagance of my desire ; for
I will not give it the serious name of design : They,
whom an enlightened taste has rendered thoroughly sen-
sible how very difficult it must be to accomplish such an
idea, will not only be the first to discern, but the most

ready

*ready to pardon those errors, into which so hazardous
an attempt may perhaps have betrayed me. I had
thoughts of introducing this performance to the Public,
by a Dissertation of considerable length on this species
of Poetry; but I forbear to indulge myself any farther
in such preliminary remarks, as the anxiety of authors
is so apt to produce, from the reflection, that, however
ingeniously written, they add little or nothing to the
success of a good Poem, and are utterly insufficient to
prevent that neglect, or oblivion, which is the inevitable
fate of a bad one.*

*In dismissing a work to my Fair Readers, which is
intended principally for their perusal, I shall only re-
commend it to their attention; and bid them farewell,
in the words of the pleasant and courteous Tassoni—*

    " *Vaglia il buon voler, s' altro non lice,*
    " *E chi la leggera, viva felice!"*

EARTHAM,
    Jan. 31, 1781.

THE

TRIUMPHS

OF

TEMPER.

CANTO I.

THE mind's foft guardian, who, tho' yet unfung,
    Infpires with harmony the female tongue,
And gives, improving every tender grace,
The fmile of angels to a mortal face;
Her powers I fing; and fcenes of mental ftrife,   5
Which form the maiden for th' accomplifh'd wife;
Where the fweet victor fees, with fparkling eyes,
Love her reward, and happinefs her prize.

                               Daughters

Daughters of beauty, who the song inspire,
To your enchanting notes attune my lyre !   10
And O ! if haply your soft hearts may gain
Or use, or pleasure from the motley strain,
Tho' formal critics, with a surly frown,
Deny your artless bard the laurel crown,
He still shall triumph, if ye deign to spread   15
Your sweeter myrtle round his honour'd head.

　　In your bright circle young SERENA grew;
A lovelier nymph the pencil never drew;
For the fond Graces form'd her easy mien,
And heaven's soft azure in her eye was seen.   20
She seem'd a rose-bud, when it first receives
The genial sun in its expanding leaves :
For now she enter'd those important years,
When the full bosom swells with hopes and fears ;
When conscious nature prompts the secret sigh,   25
And sheds sweet languor o'er the melting eye ;
When nobler toys the female heart trepan,
And dolls rejected, yield their place to man.

　　Beneath a father's care SERENA grew.;
The good SIR GILBERT, to his country true,   30

A faithful

A faithful Whig, who, zealous for the ftate,
In freedom's fervice led the loud debate ;
Yet every day, by tranfmutation rare,
Turn'd to a Tory in his elbow-chair,
And made his daughter pay, howe'er abfurd,   35
Paffive obedience to his fovereign word.

   In his domeftic fway he borrow'd aid
From prim PENELOPE, an ancient maid,
His upright fifter, confcious of her worth,
Who valued ftill her beauty, and her birth ;   40
Tho' from her birth no envied rank fhe gain'd,
And of her beauty but the ghoft remain'd ;
A reftlefs ghoft ! that with remembrance keen
Proclaim'd inceffant what it once had been ;
Delighted ftill the fteps of youth to haunt,   45
To watch the tender nymph, and warm gallant ;
And, with an eye that petrified purfuit,
Hang like the dragon o'er th' Hefperian fruit.

   Tho' ftrictly guarded by this jealous power,
The mild SERENA no reftraint could four :   50
Pure was her bofom, as the filver lake,
Ere rifing winds the ruffled water fhake,

When the bright pageants of the morning sky,
Acrofs th' expanfive mirror lightly fly,
By vernal gales in quick fucceffion driven, 55
While the clear glafs reflects the fmile of heaven.
In gay content a fportive life fhe led,
The child of Modefty, by Virtue bred :
Her light companions Innocence and Eafe :
Her hope was pleafure, and her wifh to pleafe : 60
For this, to Fafhion early rites fhe paid ;
For this, to Venus fecret vows fhe made ;
Nor held it fin to caft a private glance
O'er the dear pages of a new romance,
Eager in fiction's touching fcenes to find 65
A field to exercife her youthful mind :
The touching fcenes new energy impreft
On all the virtues of her feeling breaft.
Sweet Evelina's fafcinating power
Had firft beguil'd of fleep her midnight hour : 70
Poffeft by fympathy's enchanting fway,
She read, unconfcious of the dawning day.
The Modern Anecdote was next convey'd
Beneath her pillow by her faithful maid.

        The

The nymph, attentive as the brooding dove, 75
Por'd o'er the tender fcenes of Franzel's love :
The finking taper now grew weak and pale ;
SERENA figh'd, and dropt th' unfinifh'd tale ;
But, as warm clouds in vernal æther roll,
The foft ideas floated in her foul : 80
Free from ambitious pride, and envious care,
To love, and to be lov'd, was all her prayer :
While thefe fond thoughts her gentle mind poffefs'd,
Soft flumber fettled on her fnowy breaft.

Scarce had her radiant eyes began to clofe, 85
When to her view a friendly vifion rofe :
A fairy Phantom ftruck her mental fight,
Light as the goffamer, as æther bright ;
Array'd like Pallas was the pigmy form,
When the fage Goddefs ftills the martial ftorm. 90
Her cafque was amber, richly grac'd above
With down, collected from the callow dove :
Her burnifh'd breaft-plate, of a deeper dye,
Was once the armour of a golden fly :
A lynx's eye her little ægis fhone, 95
By fairy fpells converted into ftone,

And

And worn of old, as elfin poets sing,

By Ægypt's lovely queen, a favourite ring:

Mysterious power was in the magic toy,

To turn the frowns of care to smiles of joy. 100

Her tiny lance, whose radiance stream'd afar,

Was one bright sparkle from the bridal star.

A filmy mantle round her figure play'd,

Fine as the texture, by Arachne laid

O'er some young plant, when glittering to the view

With many an orient pearl of morning dew. 106

The Phantom hover'd o'er the conscious Fair

With such a lively smile of tender care,

As on her elfin lord Titania cast,

When first she found his angry spell was past. 110

Round her rich locks SERENA chanc'd to tie

An ample ribband of cærulean dye:

High o'er her forehead rose the graceful bow,

Whose arch commanded the sweet scene below:

The hovering Spirit view'd the tempting spot, 115

And lightly perch'd on this unbending knot;

As the fair flutterer, of Psyche's race,

Is seen to terminate her airy chace,

When,

When, pleas'd at length her quivering wings to clofe,
Fondly fhe fettles on the fragrant rofe.   120

   Now in foft notes, more mufically clear
Than ever Fairy breath'd in mortal ear,
Thefe words the vifionary voice convey'd
To the charm'd fpirit of the fleeping maid:
   " Thou darling of my care, whofe ripen'd worth
Shall fpread my empire o'er the fmiling earth ;   126
Whom Nature bleft, forbidding modifh Art
To cramp thy fpirit, or contract thy heart ;
Screen'd from thy thought, nor in thy vifions felt,
Long on thy opening mind I've fondly dwelt ;   130
In childhood's forrows brought thee quick relief,
And dry'd thy April fhowers of infant grief;
Taught thee to laugh at the malicious boy,
Who broke thy playthings with a barbarous joy,
To bear what ills the little female haunt,   135
The tefty nurfe, th' imperious governante,
And that tyrannic peft, the prying maiden aunt.
Now ripening years a nobler fcene fupply ;
For life now opens on thy fparkling eye :
Thy rifing bofom fwells with juft defire   140
Rapture to feel, and rapture to infpire :
                                   Not

Not the vain blifs, the tranfitory joys,
That childifh woman feels, in radiant toys ;
The coftly diamond, or the lighter pearl,
The maffive Nabob, or the tinfel Earl.   145
Thy heart demands, each meaner aim above,
Th' imperifhable wealth of fterling love ;
Thy wifh, to pleafe by ev'ry fofter grace
Of elegance and eafe, of form and face !
By lively fancy and by fenfe refin'd,   150
The ftronger magic of the cultur'd mind !
Thy pure ambition, and thy virtuous plan,
To fix the variable heart of man !
Short is the worfhip paid at beauty's fhrine ;
But lafting love and happinefs are mine :   155
Mine, tho' the earth's miftaken, blinded race
Defpife my influence, and my name debafe ;
Nor breathe one vow to that ætherial friend,
On whom the colours of their life depend.
But to thy innocence I'll now difplay   160
The myftic marvels of my fecret fway ;
And tell, in this thy fate-deciding hour,
My race, my name, my office, and my power.

Firft

First, hear what wonders human forms contain !
And learn the texture of the female brain ! 165
By Nature's care in curious order spread,
This living net is fram'd of tender thread ;
Fine, as thy hand, some favour'd youth to grace,
Knits with nice art to form the mimic lace.
Within the center of this fretted dome, 170
Her secret tower, her heaven-constructed home,
Soft Sensibility, sweet Beauty's soul !
Keeps her coy state, and animates the whole,
Invisible as Harmony, who springs,
Wak'd by young Zephyr, from Æolian strings : 175
Her subtle power, more delicately fine,
Dwells in each thread, and lives in every line,
Whose quick vibrations, without end, impart
Pleasure and pain to the responsive heart.
As Zephyr's breath the willing chord inspires, 180
Whispering soft music to the trembling wires,
So with fond care I regulate, unseen,
The softer movements of this nice machine ;
TEMPER my earthly name, the nurse of Love !
But call'd SOPHROSYNE in realms above ! 185

When lovely Woman, perfect at her birth,
Bleſt with her early charms the wond'ring earth,
Her ſoul, in ſweet ſimplicity array'd,
Nor ſhar'd my guidance, nor requir'd my aid.
Her tender frame, nor confident nor coy,   190
Had every fibre tun'd to gentle joy :
No vain caprices ſwell'd her pouting lip ;
No gold produc'd a mercenary trip ;
Soft innocence inſpir'd her willing kiſs,
Her love was nature, and her life was bliſs.   195
Guide of his reaſon, not his paſſion's prey,
She tam'd the ſavage, Man, who bleſs'd her ſway.
No jarring wiſhes fill'd the world with woes,
But youth was ecſtacy, and age repoſe.
   The Powers of Miſchief met, in dark Divan, 200
To blaſt theſe mighty joys of envied Man :
The Fiends, at their infernal leader's call,
Fram'd their baſe wiles in Demogorgon's hall.
In the deep center of that dreadful dome,
An helliſh cauldron boil'd with fiery foam :   205
In this wide urn the circling ſpirits threw
Ingredients harſh, and hideous to the view ;

                                        While

While the terrific mafter of the fpell
With adjurations fhook the depths of hell,
And in dark words, unmeet for mortal ear,   210
Bade the dire offspring of his art appear.
Forth from the vafe, with fullen murmurs, broke
A towering mafs of peftilential fmoke :
Emerging from this fog of thickeft night,
A Phantom fwells, by flow degrees, to fight ;   215
But ere the view can feize the forming fhape,
From the mock'd eye its lineaments efcape :
It feem'd all paffions melted into one,
Affum'd the face of all, and yet was none :
Hell ftood aghaft at its portentous mien,   220
And fhuddering Demons call'd the fpectre Spleen.
' Hie thee to earth !' its mighty mafter cried,
' O'er the vex'd globe in heavy vapours ride !
Within its center fix thy fhadowy throne !
With fhades thy fubjects, and that hell thy own ! 225
Reign there unfeen ! but let thy ftrong controul
Be hourly felt in Woman's wayward foul !
With darkeft poifons from our deep abyfs,
Taint that pure fountain of terreftrial blifs !'

C 2   Th'

Th' enormous Phantom, at this potent found,   230
Roll'd forth obedient from the vaſt profound :
The quaking Fiends recover'd from their dread,
And hell grew lighter, as the monſter fled.
But now round earth the gliding vapours run,
Blot the rich æther, and eclipſe the ſun ;   235
All Nature ſickens ; and her faireſt flower,
Enchanting Woman, feels the baneful Power :
As in her ſoul the clouds of Spleen ariſe,
The ſprightly eſſence of her beauty flies :
In youth's gay prime, in hours with rapture warm,
Love looks aſtoniſh'd on her altering form :   241
To pleaſing frolics, and enchanting wiles,
Life-darting looks, and ſoul-ſubduing ſmiles,
Dark whims ſucceed : thick-coming fancies fret ;
The ſullen paſſion, and the haſty pet :   245
The ſwelling lip, the tear-diſtended eye,
The peeviſh queſtion, the perverſe reply ;
The moody humour, that, like rain and fire,
Blends cold diſguſt with unſubdu'd deſire,
Flies what it loves, and, petulantly coy,   250
Feigns proud abhorrence of the proffer'd joy :

                                        For

For Nature's artlefs aim, the wifh to pleafe
By genuine modefty, and fimple eafe,
Fafhion's pert tricks the crowded brain opprefs
With all the poor parade of tawdry drefs :   255
The fickly bofom pants for noife and fhow,
For every bauble, and for every beau ;
The voice, that health made harmony, difowns
That native charm for languor's mimic tones ;
And feigns difeafe, till, feeling what it feigns,   260
Its fancied maladies are real pains.
Such, and a thoufand ftill fuperior woes,
From Spleen's new empire o'er the earth arofe :
Each fimple dictate of the foul forgot,
Then firft was form'd the mercenary plot ;   265
And beauty practis'd that pernicious art,
The art of angling for an old man's heart ;
Tho' crawling to his bride with tottering knees,
His words were dotage, and his love difeafe.
From fex to fex this bafe contagion ran,   270
And gold grew beauty in the eyes of man :
Courtfhip was traffic : and the married life
But one loud jangle of inceffant ftrife.

C 3

The

The gentle Sprite, who, on his radiant car,
Shines the mild regent of the evening-ſtar,   275
And joys from thence thoſe genial rays to ſhed,
That lead the bridegroom to the nuptial bed,
While earth's new ills his friendly ſoul abſorb,
From Cynthia call'd me to his kindred orb;
And, eager to redreſs the woes of man,   280
The brilliant Son of Veſper thus began:
' Thou ſofteſt Being of th' ætherial kind,
Be thy benignant cares no more confin'd
To ſmooth the ruffled plume of Zephyr's wing,
To guard from cruel froſt the infant ſpring,   285
To drive groſs atoms from the rays of noon,
Or chaſe the halo from the vapouriſh moon!
Thy friendly nature will not now deny
To quit for nobler toils thy native ſky;
Thou feeſt how Spleen's infernal vapours roll   290
Acroſs the ſweet ſerene of woman's ſoul;
And earth, which darkens as her beauties fade,
Muſt grow a ſecond hell without thy aid:
Take then thy ſtation! fix thy nobler reign
O'er thoſe fine chords, that form the female brain,

4   That

That us'd, ere injur'd by the ruſt of Spleen,   296
To fill with harmony the human ſcene !
Go ! left her touch their tender tones deſtroy,
Teach them to vibrate to thy notes of joy !
Go ! and reſtore, by ſtilling mental ſtrife,   300
Health to faint love, and happineſs to life ! '
So ſpake that friend of man, who lights above
His heavenly lamp of Hymenæal love :
In his juſt aim my kindred ſpirit join'd,
And flew obedient to the charge aſſign'd.   305
Hence, as the bias ſways th' unconſcious bowl,
I long unſeen have ſway'd the careleſs ſoul ;
Tho' oft I feel my power by Spleen ſubdu'd,
In the ſhrill vixen, and the ſullen prude,
In ſome fair forms my ſoft dominion grows,   310
Like fragrance, riſing from the opening roſe :
Still I preſerve, in many a lovely face,
That gay good-humour, and that conſtant grace,
Which heavenly Powers united to infold
In perfect Woman's new-created mould ;   315
When Nature, in her infant beauty bleſt,
The laſt and lovelieſt of her works careſt.

But of thofe nymphs, who, delicately fair,
Draw their foft graces from my forming care,
My young SERENA fhines her peers above,   320
Pride of my hopes, and darling of my love,
Hence I to thee fuch myfteries unfold,
As Man's pedantic eye fhall ne'er behold ;
Whofe narrow fcience, tho' it proudly boaft
To pierce the fky, and count the ftarry hoft,   325
Sees not the lucid band of airy Powers,
Who flutter round him in his fecret hours :
But if to me, thy guardian now difplay'd,
Thy duteous orifons are juftly paid,
Thou to thofe realms fhalt pafs with me thy guide,
Where Spleen's pale victims, after death, refide ; 331
Then to that orb, in vifion fhalt thou rife,
Unfeen by mortal aftronomic eyes,
Where I—but firft let me thy foul prepare
To meet our fecret foe's infidious fnare !   335
'Tis my fond purpofe in thy form to fhow
The fweeteft model of my fkill below :
A youth I deftine to thy dear embrace,
Crown'd with each mental charm, and manly grace,

With

whom thy innocence, fecure from ftrife,   340
p the beauteous joys of blamelefs life.
d I obferve thy little heart begin
afk, what charms the mighty prize may win:
ut know, tho' Elegance herfelf be feen
To guide thy motion, and to form thy mien;   345
Tho' Beauty o'er thy filial cheek diffufe
The foft enchantment of her rofeate hues,
Not from their favour fhall this glory rife!
TEMPER fhall fingly gain the fplendid prize:
The fudden conqueft fhall be mine alone,   350
And Love with tranfport fhall my triumph own.
Such are my hopes; but I with pain relate
What hard conditions are annex'd by fate:
As chemic fires, that patient labour blows,
Draw the rich perfume from the Perfian rofe, | 355
So muft thou form, by fiery toils refin'd,
The living effence of thy fweeter mind.
Dimly I fee, on Deftiny's dull glafs,
Three dangerous trials 'tis thy doom to pafs;
And oh! if once forgetful of my power,   360
Good-humour fail thee in the fateful hour,

                                    Farewell

Farewell thofe joys, that wait the happy wife !
Farewell the vifion of unclouded life !

Fain would my love thy fecret perils fhow,
Which fate allows not even me to know :   365
In Spleen's dark court a thoufand agents dwell,
Who bind her victims in the wayward fpell ;
Perchance three prime fupporters of her fway,
The bufieft of her fiends, may crofs thy way :
Stern Contradiction, her ill-favour'd child,   370
Of fierce demeanor, and of fpirit wild,
Bane of delight ! and horror of the fex !
His plan to puzzle, and his pride to vex !—
Or Scandal, filthy hag ! who blindly limps
Round the wide earth, fupported by her imps,   375
Her inky demons, who delight to print
Her bafe fuggeftion, and her envious hint :—
Or groundlefs Jealoufy, pert changeling ! born
Of amorous Vanity, and angry Scorn,
Whofe bitter taunts with public infult dare   380
Bafely to wound the unoffending fair,
Proud the fweet joys of innocence to crufh,
And fpread o'er beauty's cheek the burning blufh.
                              Whether

Whether thefe kindred fiends, or one or all,

Shall aim thy airy fpirit to enthrall, 385

Are points, my fondnefs tries in vain to reach;

But truft my caution! and beware of each!

   Left to thy lively mind my words may feem

The vain chimera of a common dream,

By one unqueftionable fign be taught 390

To prize my prefence in thy waking thought!

An azure ribband, on thy toilet thrown,

Shall make the magic of my empire known:

On this thy fportive needle tried its powers,

And filver fpangles form'd the mimic flowers; 395

On thefe my love fhall breathe a fecret charm;

With this, my cæftus, thy foft bofom arm!

Above it let the decent tucker rife,

To hide the myftic band from mortal eyes! |

When Spleen's dark Powers would teach that breaft

    to fwell, 400

This guardian cincture fhall thofe Powers repel:

As the touch'd talifman, more fwift than thought,

To fave her charge, th' Arabian Fairy brought;

So fhall this zone, if juftly I'm obey'd,

Bring my foft fpirit to thy certain aid. 405

                    In

In Love's great name obferve this high beheft!
Revere my power—Be gentle, and be bleft!"

　Here the kind Sprite her friendly counfel clos'd,
And lightly vanifh'd—Still SERENA doz'd;
Still in fweet trance fhe fondly feem'd to hear　　410
The foft perfuafion vibrate in her ear.
But waking now far different notes fhe found;
Lefs pleafing echoes in her chamber found;
For now the heralds of the London day
Sing their loud mattins in th' uncrowded way;　415
Th' impatient milk-maid now, with early din,
Screams to the rattle of her pail of tin;
With fweep's faint cry, and, lateft of the crew,
The deep-ton'd mufic of the murmuring Jew.

END OF THE FIRST CANTO.

CANTO

CANTO II.

YE radiant nymphs! whofe opening eyes convey
    Warmth to the world, and luftre to the day!
Think what o'erfhadowing clouds may crofs your
        brain,
Before thofe lovely lids fhall clofe again!
What funds of patience twelve long hours may afk, 5
When cold Difcretion claims her daily tafk!
Ah think betimes! and, while your morning care
Sheds foreign odours o'er your fragrant hair,
Tinge your foft fpirit with that mental fweet,
Which may not be exhal'd by paffion's heat; 10
But charm the fenfe, with undecaying power,
Thro' every chance of each diurnal hour!
O! might you all perceive your toilets crown'd
With fuch cofmetics as SERENA found!
For, to the warning vifion fondly true, 15
Now the quick fair-one to the toilet flew:

                                    With

With keen delight her ravifh'd eye furvey'd
The myftic ribband on her mirror laid :
Bright fhone the azure as Aurora's car,
And every fpangle feem'd a living ftar.   20
With fportive grace the fmiling damfel preft
The guardian cincture to her fnowy breaft,
More lovely far than Juno, when fhe ftrove
To look moft lovely in the eyes of Jove ;
And willing Venus lent her every power, .   25
That fheds enchantment o'er the amorous hour :
For fpells more potent on this band were thrown,
Than Venus boafted in her beauteous zone.
Her dazzling cæftus could àlone infpire
The fudden impulfe of fhort-liv'd defire :   30
Thefe finer threads with lafting charms are fraught,
Here lies the tender, but unchanging thought,
Silence, that wins, where eloquence is vain,
And tones, that harmonize the madd'ning brain,
Soft fighs, that anger cannot hear, and live,   35
And fmiles, that tell, how truly they forgive ;
And lively grace, whofe gay diffufive light
Puts the black phantoms of the brain to flight,

Whofe

Whofe cheering powers thro' every period laft,
And make the prefent happy as the paft.   40
    Such fecret charms this richer zone poffeft,
Whofe flowers, now fparkling on SERENA's breaft,
Give, tho' unfeen thofe fwelling orbs they bind,
Smiles to her face, and beauty to her mind:
For now, obfervant of the Sprite's beheft,   45
The nymph conceals them by her upper veft:
Safe lies the fpell, no mortal may defcry,
Not keen PENELOPE's all-piercing eye;
Who conftant, as the fteps of morn advance,
Surveys the houfhold with a fearching glance,   50
And entering now, with all her ufual care,
Reviews the chamber of the youthful fair.
Beneath the pillow, not completely hid,
The novel lay—She faw—fhe feiz'd—fhe chid:
With rage and glee her glaring eye-balls flafh,   55
Ah wicked age! fhe cries, ah filthy trafh!
From the firft page my juft abhorrence fprings;
For modern anecdotes are monftrous things:
Yet will I fee what dangerous poifons lurk,
To taint thy youth, in this licentious work.   60

She

She faid : and rudely from the chamber rufh'd,
Her pallid cheek with expectation flufh'd,
With ardent hope her eager fpirit fhook,
Vain hope ! to banquet on a lufcious book.
So if a prieft, of the Arabian fect,   65
In Turkifh hands forbidden wine detect,
The facred muffulman, with pious din,
Arraigns the culprit, and proclaims the fin,
Curfes with holy zeal th' inflaming juice,
But curfing takes it for his fecret ufe.   70

The gay SERENA, with unruffled mind,
The pleafing novel, thus unread, refign'd.
The vifion on her foul fuch virtue left,
She only fmil'd at the provoking theft ;
The teazing incident fhe deem'd a jeft,   75
Nor felt the zone grow tighter on her breaft.

Now in full charms defcends the finifh'd fair,
For now the morning banquet claims her care ;
Already at the board, with viands pil'd,
Her fire impatient fits, and chides his tardy child. 80
On his imperial lips rude hunger reigns,
And keener politics ufurp his brains :

But

But when her love-inſpiring voice he hears;
When the ſoft magic of her ſmile appears;
In that glad moment he at once forgets   85
His empty ſtomach, and the nation's debts:
He bends to Nature's more divine controul,
And only feels the Father in his ſoul.
Quick to his hand behold her now preſent
The Indian liquor of celeſtial ſcent !   90
Not with more grace the nectar'd cup is given
By roſe-lipp'd Hebe to the lord of heaven.
While her fair hands a freſh libation pour,
Faſhion's loud thunder wakes the ſounding door.
The light SERENA to the window ſprings,   95
On curioſity's amuſive wings:
Her quick eyes ſparkle with ſurpriſe, to ſee
The glories of a golden vis-à-vis:
Its glittering tablet gleam'd with mimic pearl,
And the rich coronet announc'd an earl.   100
The good old knight grew ſomewhat proud to hear
Of this new viſit from the early peer:
SERENA recollects the viſion's truth,
And fluttering, hopes it is the promis'd youth:

VOL. V.   D   PENELOPE

PENELOPE from her high chamber peeps;   105
There her unfinifh'd charms fhe coyly keeps;
With fage referve her modefty abhorr'd
To fhew her morning face before a lord.

The peer alights : the well-rang'd vaffals bawl
His founding title thro' the fpacious hall,   110
Till in the deep faloon's extremeft bound.
Th' ear-tickling words, "LORD FILLIGREE,"
          refound.

As when great Hector, fetting war apart,
Advanc'd to parley, with his fpear athwart,
The Greeks beheld him with a ftill delight;   115
And filent reverence ftopt the rifing fight;
With fuch refpect, but unchaftis'd by fear,
SIR GILBERT and the nymph firft meet the peer;
And, while his morning compliments commence,
The flighted breakfaft ftands in cold fufpence,   120
But far unlike to Hector's ruder grace
His modern ftature, and his modifh face!
Nor lefs he differs from thofe barons old,
Whofe arms are blazon'd on his car of gold;
Whofe proftrate caftle guarded once the lands,   125
Where, fpruce in motley pride, his villa ftands,

                                        By

By Taſte erected, in her trimmeſt mode,
Her muſhroom ſtructure, and her quaint abode.

　　As the neat daiſy to the ſun's broad flower,
As the French boudoir to the Gothic tower,　　130
Such is the peer, whom faſhion much admires,
Compar'd in perſon to his ancient ſires :
For their broad ſhoulder, and their brawny calf,
Their coarſe, loud language, and their coarſer laugh,
His finer form, more elegantly ſlim,　　135
Diſplays the faſhionable length of limb :
With foreign ſhrugs his country he regards,
And her lean tongue with foreign words he lards ;
While Gallic Graces, who correct his ſtyle,
Forbid his mirth to paſs beyond a ſmile.　　140
As the nice workman in the wooden trade,
Hides his coarſe ground, with fineſt woods o'erlaid,
Thus our young lord, with faſhion's phraſe refin'd,
Fineer'd the mean interior of his mind :
And hence, in courteſy's ſoft luſtre ſeen,　　145
His ſpirit ſhone, as graceful as his mien.
The artleſs fair, on faſhion's kind report,
Thought him the mirror of a matchleſs court :

　　　　　　D 2　　　　　　　Much

Much fhe his drefs, his language much obferves,
Whofe finer accents prove his feeling nerves.   150
Her fancy now the deftin'd lover fpies,
But her free heart abjures the quick furmife ;
Yet as he fpoke, at every flattering word
The vifion's promife to her thought recurr'd.
Far more parental pride contrives to blind   155
The good SIR GILBERT's more-experienc'd mind,
Who fondly faw, and at the profpect fmil'd,
A future countefs in his favourite child.
But what new flutterings fhook SERENA's breaft,
What hopes and fears the modeft nymph oppreft, 160
When with a fimpering fmile, and foft regard,
The peer difplay'd a mirth-expreffive card,
Where the gay Graces, in a fportive band,
Shew the fweet art of Cipriani's hand ;
Where, in their train, his airy Cupids throng,   165
And laughing drag a comic mafk along !
" We," cries my lord, with felf-fufficient joy,
Twirling, with lordly airs, the graceful toy,
" We, who poffefs true fcience, we, who give
The world a leffon in the art to live,   170

We

We for the fair a fplendid fête defign,
And pay our homage thus at Beauty's fhrine."
He fpoke ; and fpeaking, to the blufhing maid,
With modifh eafe, th' inviting card convey'd,
Where Mirth announc'd her mafque-devoted hour
In characters intwin'd with many a flower : 176
The blufhing maid, with eyes of quick defire,
View'd it, and felt her little foul on fire ;
For of all fcenes fhe had not yet furvey'd,
Her heart moft panted for a mafquerade : 180
But her gay hopes increafing terrors drown,
And dread forebodings of her father's frown.
In mute fufpence to read his thought fhe tries,
And ftrongly pleads with her prevailing eyes,
Her eyes, for doubt enchain'd her modeft tongue, 185
While on his fovereign word her pleafure hung.
With fuch a tender, and perfuafive air
Of foft endearment, and of anxious care,
Thetis attended from th' almighty fire
His fateful anfwer to her fond defire : 190
The good old knight, like the Olympian god,
Bleft the fair fuppliant with his gracious nod ;

D 3

Her

Her lively fpirit the kind fignal took,
And her glad heart in every fibre fhook.
The party fettled, it imports not how,   195
The peer politely made his parting bow;
The nymph, with eyes that fparkled joyous fire,
Kifs'd the round cheek of her complying fire,
Then fwiftly flew, and fummon'd to her aid
Th' important counfel of her favourite maid,   200
To vent her joy, and, as the moments prefs,
To fix that firft of points, a fancy-drefs.

Quick as the poet's eyes o'er nature fly,
Piercing the deep, or traverfing the fky,
With fuch light fpeed her fond ideas glance   205
O'er play and poem, ftory and romance,
While all the characters, fhe e'er has read,
Flafh on her brain, and fill her bufy head.

Now in Diana's form fhe hopes to meet
A fond Endymion fighing at her feet;   210
Now her proud thought terreftrial pomp affumes,
And Dian's crefcent yields to Indian plumes;
Now, in the habit of the Grecian ifles,
She hears fome Ofman fuing for her fmiles,

And

And fees his foul that blaze of drefs outfhine,   215
Whofe wealth impoverifh'd a diamond-mine;
Now fimpler charms her quick attention draw,
The rofe-crown'd bonnet, and the hat of ftraw,
A village-maid fhe feems, in neat attire,
A faithful fhepherd now her fole defire.   220
Thus, as new figures in her fancy throng,
" She's every thing by ftarts, and nothing long ;"
But, in the fpace of one revolving hour,
Flies thro' all ftates of poverty and power,
All forms, on whom her veering mind can pitch, 225
Sultana, gipfy, goddefs, nymph, and witch.
At length, her foul with Shakefpeare's magic fraught,
The wand of Ariel fixt her roving thought;
Ariel's light graces all her heart poffefs,
And Jenny's order'd to prepare the drefs.   230
It feems already bought, with fond applaufe ;
An azure tiffue, and a filver gauze ;
Too-foon, alas ! that garb of heavenly hue
The ready mercer flafhes to her view.
Ah blind to fate ! how oft the youthful belle   235
Feels her gay heart at fight of tiffue fwell !

And

And thinks the fashionable, silk must prove
Her robe of triumph, and a spell to love !
To thee, sweet maid, whose pleasure-darting eyes
Joy in this favourite vest, an hour shall rise,   240
When thou shalt hate the silk so fondly sought,
And wish thy silver-spotted gauze unbought * :
For busy Spleen thy trial now prepares ;
Darkly she forms her unsuspected snares,
And, keen to raise her pleasure-killing storm,   245
Assumes PENELOPE's congenial form.
In that prim shape, which all the graces shun,
See the sour fiend to good SIR GILBERT run !
Where, deeply pondering the public debt,
Silent he muses o'er a new gazette !   250
Ent'ring, she view'd, with eyes of envious spite,
The card, that spoke the masque-devoted night ;

---

* Nescia mens hominum fati sortisque futuræ,
  Et servare modum, rebus sublata secundis.
  Turno tempus erit, magno cum optaverit emptum
  Intactum Pallanta, et cum spolia ista diemque
  Oderit.   ÆNEID. X. V. 501. & seq.

Eager

Eager fhe darted on the graceful toy,
And, fiercely pointing to each naked boy,
" Canft thou," fhe cried, in a difcordant fcream, 255
That rous'd the politician from his dream,
While with her voice the echoing chamber rings,
" * Say ! canft thou fuffer thefe flagitious things ?
Are thefe devices to thy daughter brought,
That wake fuch grofs impurity of thought ? 260
In vain are all the prudent words I preach,
The modeft maxims that I ftrive to teach ;
By foolifh fondnefs of your fenfe beguil'd,
You ftill indulge, and fpoil the flippant child :
For me, whate'er I fay is deem'd abfurd ; 265
She fcorns my fage advice :—but mark my word,
If to this ball you let the hoyden run,
Your power is ended, and the girl undone,"
 The patriot knight, by interruption vext,
In his political purfuits perplext, 270
While he with wrath th' intruding Mifchief eyed,
Stern to the falfe PENELOPE replied :

* Ζευ πατερ, η νεμεσιζη, οξων ταδι καρτερα εργα, &c.
                    ILIAD ι. v. 872. & feq.
                        " Go !

" Go ! teazing prude, ceafe in my ears to vent

Thy envious pride, and peevifh difcontent !

To me of prudence canft thou vainly boaft ?   275

Of all my houfhold, thou haft plagu'd me moft :

The joys thou blameft are thy dear delight,

By day the vifit, and the ball by night :

And, tho' too old a lover to trepan,

Thy midnight dream, thy morning thought, is man.

Wert thou lefs clofely to my blood allied,   281

Thou fhould'ft, to cure thee of thy canting pride,

Be fent to figh alone o'er purling brooks,

Scold village maids, and croak to croaking rooks."

  He fpoke indignant : the fly fiend withdrew,   285

Nor inly griev'd ; for well her force fhe knew.

As Indian females, in a jealous hour,

Of fecret poifon try the fubtleft power,

Which fure, tho' flow, corrodes th' unconfcious prey,

And ends its triumph on a diftant day :   290

Thus the departing Fury left behind

Her venom, latent in SIR GILBERT's mind.

The hidden mifchief tho' no eye obferves,

He feels it fretting on his alter'd nerves ;

                       But

But the kind habit of his healthy foul   295
Still ftruggled hard againft its bafe controul.
Now Spleen's dark vapours, in his bofom hid,
Prompt him the promis'd pleafure to forbid ;
Now Love's foft pleadings that dire thought deftroy,
And fave the bloffom of his daughter's joy ;   300
Her envious aunt now ferves him for a jeft,
And gay good-humour reaffumes his breaft.

While Spleen's dark power now finks, and now
          revives,
At length the day, th' important day, arrives,
Which in his breaft muft end the clofe debate,   305
And fix the colour of SERENA's fate.

Now comes the hour, when the convivial knight
Waits to begin the dinner's chearful rite ;
His fond heart ever, with a father's pride,
Joys to behold his darling at his fide ;   310
But moft the abfence of her fmile he feels
In the gay feafon of his focial meals :
Hence, while for her the rich repaft attends,
His hafty fummons to the nymph he fends :

The

The happy nymph superior cares induce 315
To risk his anger by a rash excuse:
She craves his pardon; but, for time distrest,
She still is busy on her magic vest;
To range her diamonds in a sparkling zone,
She begs to snatch her scanty meal alone. 320

    The knight in sullen state begins to dine:
Spleen, like a harpy, flutters o'er his wine:
Invisible she poisons every dish,
Tinging with gall his mutton, fowl, and fish.
The more he eats, the more perverse he grows; 325
For as his hunger sunk, his choler rose.
The cloth remov'd, he cries, with vapours sick,
The pears are mellow, and the port is thick;
Tho' nicer fruit Pomona never knew,
And his rich wine surpass'd the ruby's hue! 330

    A thousand times his dizzy brain revolves
A stern command: now doubts, and now resolves
To bid the nymph descend, and, disarray'd,
Quit her dear project of of the masquerade:
As oft kind nature to his heart recurr'd, 335
And love parental stopt the cruel word.

                                      Mean

Mean time, unconfcious of the brooding ftorm,
The nymph exults in her improving form :
Gay is her fmile, as thofe the queen of love
Darts on the Graces in her court above,　　　340
While they contrive, with love-infpiring cares,
New modes of beauty for the robe fhe wears.
At length, each duty of the toilet paft,
The glance of triumph on the mirror caft,
Now the light wand our finifh'd Ariel arms ;　345
Glad Jenny glories in her lady's charms ;
And gives full utterance, as fhe fmooths her veft,
To the fweet bodings of SERENA's breaft.

O ! lovely bias of the female foul !
Which trembling points to pleafure's diftant pole ; 350
Which with fond truft on flattering hope relies,
O'erleaps each peril, that in profpect lies,
And fpringing to the goal, anticipates the prize !
Such was SERENA's fear-difcarding ftate ;
Her eye beheld not the dark frowns of fate :　355
She only faw, the combat all forgot,
The triumph promis'd as her glorious lot.

Now,

Now, eager to display her light attire,
The sprightly damsel seeks her sullen sire;
His gloomy brow with sportive air she kist: 360
Ah! how could Spleen that magic lip resist?
That voice, whose melting music might assuage
The scorpion Anger's self-tormenting rage?
For ne'er did nature to a sire's embrace
Present a filial form of softer grace;   365
Or fancy view a shape of lovelier kind
In the bright mirror of her Shakespeare's mind.

The sulky fiend, in spite of all her art,
Had now been banish'd from the father's heart;
But that, resolv'd her utmost force to try,   370
She summon'd to her aid her old ally,
The fiery demon, temper-troubling Gout;
Who sinks the lively, and appals the stout;
Who now, assisting Spleen's malignant aim,
Shoots in quick throbbings through SIR GIL-
        BERT's frame.   375
Thus sorely pester'd by a double foe,
Galling his giddy brain, and burning toe,

3   The

The tefty knight, with ftern and fullen air,
Denounc'd his humour to the fhudd'ring fair:
" Go change your drefs! give up this vain delight!
I will not hear of mafquerades to-night;   381
Your chaperone's inform'd fhe need not wait,
So change your drefs! and fit with me fedate."

   As the proud dame, whofe avaricious glee
Built golden caftles in the rich South Sea,   385.
Gaz'd on her broker, when he told her firft
Her wealth was vanifh'd, and the bubble burft:
So gaz'd the nymph, hearing her fire deftroy
Her airy palace of ideal joy.
Firft her fond thoughts to flattering doubt incline,
And deem the harfh command no fix'd defign, |391
But the quick fally of a peevifh word,
That love revokes, the moment it is heard:
Or haply mirth, in mimic wrath expreft,
A feign'd forbiddance utter'd but in jeft: 395.
To this fhort hope, her finking fpirit clung,
To fee his foftening eyes refute his tongue.
Ah fruitlefs hope! for there fhe cannot find
The well-known fignals of the friendly mind.

                           Stern

Stern contradiction, with the frown of fate,   400
On his dark vifage reign'd in fullen ftate ;
Felt in each feature, in each accent fhown,
Lower'd in his look, and thunder'd in his tone.
Hence the warm bofom of the lively fair
Now fhivers with the chill of blank defpair :   405
Now difappointment's thick'ning fhadows roll
A cloud of horror o'er the darken'd foul ;
And fancy, in a fick delirium toft,
Gives double value to each pleafure loft.
The blafted joys, fhe labours to forget,   410
Rufh on her mind, and waken keen regret :
Her cheek turns pale—the tear prepares to ftart,
And palpitation heaves her fwelling heart.
But here, SOPHROSYNE ! thy guardian aid
Saves from her potent foe the finking maid.   415
Her bofom, into ftrong emotions thrown,
Now feels the preffure of thy friendly zone.
Swift thy kind cautions to her foul recur,
More quick to cancel faults, than prone to err.
As the rough fwell of the infurgent tides   420
By the mild impulfe of the moon fubfides :

So

So, by her myſtic monitor repreſt,
The flood of paſſion leaves her lighten'd breaſt,
From her clear brain each cloudy vapour flies,
And joy's bright ray rekindles in her eyes.   425
Reviving gaiety full luſtre ſpread
O'er all her features, and with ſmiles ſhe ſaid:
" Let others drive to pleaſure's diſtant home !
Be mine the dearer joy to pleaſe at home !"
Scarce had ſhe ſpoke, when ſhe with ſportive eaſe
Preſt her piano-forte's fav'rite keys,   431
O'er ſofteſt notes her rapid fingers ran,
Sweet prelude to the Air ſhe thus began !

> SOPHROSYNE ! thou guard unſeen !
>   Whoſe delicate controul   435
> Can turn the diſcord of chagrin
>   To harmony of ſoul !
> Above the lyre, the lute above,
>   Be mine thy melting tone,
> Which makes the peace of all we love   440
>   The baſis of our own !

So fung the nymph, not uninfpir'd: the fprite
Invok'd fo fondly in the myftic rite,
With richeft mufic fwell'd her warbling throat,
And gave new fweetnefs to her fweeteft note. 445
As when the feraph Uriel firft begun
His carol to the new-created fun,
The facred echo fhook the vaft profound,
And chaos perifh'd at the potent found:
So, at the magic of SERENA's ftrain, 450
Spleen vanifh'd from her fire's chaotic brain;
Whofe fibres, lighten'd of that load, rejoice
In the dear accents of her dulcet voice.
Much he inclines his mandate to recall,
And fend the fair-one to the promis'd ball; 455
But ftubborn pride forbids him to revoke
The folemn fentence, which ill-humour fpoke.
Still, confcious of her power, the nymph prolongs
The foft enchantment of her foothing fongs;
Which his fond mind in firm attention keep, 460
To his fixt hour of fupper and of fleep:
This now arriv'd, the knight, retiring, fhed
A double bleffing on his darling's head;

And

And with unusual exultation prest
His lovely child to his parental breast.   465

   Thus while to rest the happy sire withdrew,
The nymph, more happy, to her chamber flew;
And, Jenny now dismiss'd, the grateful fair
Breathes to her guardian Sprite this tender prayer:
"Thou kind preserver! whose attentive zeal   470
Gives me in this contended hour to feel
That dearest pleasure of a soul refin'd,
The triumph of the self-corrected mind;
If, happy in the strength thy smiles impart,
I own thy favour in no thankless heart,   475
Still let me view thy form, so justly dear!
-Still in kind visions to these eyes appear!
Thy friendly dictates teach me to fulfil!
·And let thy aid avert each future ill!"

   While fond devotion taught her thus to speak,
The soft down sinks beneath her lovely cheek,   481
And settling on her lips, that sweetly close,
Silence, enamour'd, lulls her to repose.

CANTO III.

YE kind tranſporters of th' excurſive ſoul !
  Ye viſions ! that, when night enwraps the pole,
The lively wanderer to new worlds convey,
Eſcaping from her heavy houſe of clay,
How could the gentle ſpirit, foe to ſtrife,   5
Bear without you this coil of waking life ?
Its grief-embitter'd cares, its joyleſs mirth,
And all the flat realities of earth ?
Sweet phantoms ! you the glowing hope inſpire,
You give to beauty charms, to fancy fire,   10
When, ſoaring like the eagle's kindred frame,
The poet dreams of everlaſting fame ;
Or, tickled by the feather of the dove,
The ſofter virgin dreams of endleſs love.
There was a time, when fortune's bright decrees 15
Were ſeen to realize ſuch dreams as theſe :

                        Now

Now dangerous vifions the fond mind decoy
Vainly to pant for unexifting joy,
While belles and bards with mournful fighs exclaim,
Mortality has feiz'd both Love and Fame.   20

 Ah fair SERENA, might the boaft be ours
To clear from fuch a charge thefe heavenly powers !
Bleft ! might thy bard deferve in Fame to fee
A guard as faithful, as Love proves to thee !
Bleft ! if that airy being gild his life,   25
Who fav'd thee trembling on the brink of ftrife,
And now, kind prompter of thy nightly dream,
Fill'd thy rapt fpirit with her facred beam !
For foon as flumber fet thy foul at large,
Thy Guardian Power revifited her charge ;   30
And, lightly hovering o'er th' illumin'd bed,
Thus with fond fmiles of approbation faid :
" Well haft thou paft, fweet maid, one trying
   fcene,
One fiery ordeal of the tyrant Spleen :
Thus, my SERENA, may thy force fuftain   35
Each harder trial, that may yet remain !
Againft the fiend to fortify thy foul,
By ufeful knowledge of her dark controul,

    E 3   I come

I come to fhow thee, what no mortal eye,
Save thine, was e'er permitted to defcry;　　40
The realms, where Spleen's infernal agents goad
The ghoftly tenants of her drear abode.
Now fummon all thy ftrength ! throw fear afide,
And firmly truft in thy æthereal guide !"

　She fpoke : and thro' the night's furrounding fhade
Th' obedient nymph, not unappall'd, convey'd;　　46
Thro' long, long tracts of darknefs, on they paft
With fpeed, that ftruck the trembling maid aghaft,
Till now, recovering by degrees, fhe found
Her foft foot prefs upon the folid ground.　　50
Encourag'd by her guide, at length fhe tries
To fearch the gloomy fcene, with anxious eyes.

　* " Thro' me ye pafs to Spleen's terrific dome,
Thro' me, to Difcontent's eternal home :

　　　　* Per me fi va nella citta dolente,
　　　　　Per me fi va nell' eterno dolore,
　　　　　Per me fi va tra la perduta gente,
　　　　　*　*　*　*　*　*　*　*
　　　　　Lafciate ogni fperanza, voi ch' intrate,
　　　　Quefte parole di colore ofcuro
　　　　　Vid' io feritte al fommo d'una porta.

　　　　　　　　　DANTE, Inferno. 3.

　　　　　　　　　　　Thro'

Thro' me, to thofe, who fadden'd human life,   55
By fullen humour or vexatious ftrife ;
And here, thro' fcenes of endlefs vapours hurl'd,
Are punifh'd in the forms they plagued the world ;
Juftly they feel no joy, who none beftow,
All ye who enter, every hope forego !"   60
O'er an arch'd cavern, rough with horrid ftone,
On which a feeble light, by flafhes, fhone,
Thefe characters, that chill'd her foul with dread,
SERENA, fixt in filent wonder, read.
As fhe began to fpeak, her voice was drown'd   65
By the fhrill echo of far other found :
Forth from the portal lamentable cries
Of wailing infants, without number, rife.
Compaffion to this poor and piteous flock
Led the foft maid ftill nearer to the rock.   70
The pining band within fhe now efpied,
And, touch'd with tender indignation, cried,
" How could thefe little forms, of life fo brief,
Deferve this dire abode of lafting grief ?"
" —Well may thy gentle heart be fore concern'd   75
At fight fo moving," the mild Sprite return'd :

" Thou

" Thou feeſt in thoſe, whoſe wailings wound thy
    ears,
The puny progeny of modern peers :
Their ſires, by avarice or ambition led,
Aliens to love, approach'd the nuptial bed ;   80
With proud indifference, and with cold diſtaſte,
Their homely brides reluctantly embrac'd,
And by ſuch union gave diſaſtrous birth
To theſe poor pale incumbrances of earth,
Who, bred in vanity, with pride their dower, 85
Were Spleen's ſure victims from their natal hour,
And in their ſplendid cradles pul'd and pin'd,
Till Fate their ill-ſpun thread of life untwin'd,
And to this veſtibule convey'd their ghoſts,
To form the van-guard of th' infernal hoſts.   90
But let not pity's ineffectual charm
Impede thy progreſs, or thy ſtrength diſarm !
Follow and fear not ! guarded by my care
From all the phantoms that around thee glare."

   She ſpoke ; and enter'd, ere the nymph replied, 95
A paſs, that open'd in the cavern's ſide,
Low, dark, and rocky—with her body bent,
SERENA follow'd down the dire deſcent.

          A ſudden

A fudden light foon ftruck her dazzled view;
But 'twas a light of fuch infernal hue,   100
As double horror to the darknefs gave,
With dread reflection from a dufky wave.
Round a black water tatter'd fpectres ftand,
With each a tiny taper in its hand;
Fierce mendicants! who ftrive fome alms to win 105
From the fair wanderer, with inceffant din.
The guardian Spirit faw SERENA grieve,
To hear of wants fhe knew not to relieve;
And to the generous nymph in pity cries:
" The gulf of Indolence before us lies,   .   110
O'er whofe dull flood, to which no bank is feen,
A boat muft waft thee to the dome of Spleen.
Thefe pallid figures, that around thee prefs,
And haunt thee with importunate diftrefs,
On earth were beggars of each different clafs,   115
Tho' blended here in one promifcuous mafs.
The poor, who fpurn'd kind induftry's controul,
The rich, who begg'd from penury of foul:
Both by their abject pride alike debas'd,
Blafphem'd that nature, which they both difgrac'd,
                                                    And,

And, hither by the fullen fiend convey'd,   121
Here ftill they ply their ineffectual trade ;
In chafe of each new paffenger they run,
Condemn'd to beg from all, to gain by none.
But from thefe wretches turn thy fruitlefs care ! 125
Behold the gulf before thee, and beware !
Nor touch the ftream, which mortal fenfe o'ercomes,
And by its baleful charm the foul benumbs !"
" —Can mortal pafs !" the fhudd'ring nymph re-
        plied,
" This fullen, flow, unnavigable tide,   130
In whofe black current this enormous mound
Of fhapelefs ftone appears, this horrid bound,
That feems an everlafting guard to keep
O'er the dull waters, that beneath it creep ?"

    While yet fhe fpoke, with a refounding fhock, 135
Forth from the arch of the impending rock,
Which o'er the murmuring eddy hung fo low,
The lazy river fcarce had room to flow,
Of rude conftruction, and in rougheft plight,
A boat now iffued to SERENA's fight ;   140
An empty boat, that flowly to the fhore
Advanc'd, without the aid of fail or oar ;

                                      Self-mov'd

Self-mov'd it feem'd, but foon the nymph beheld
A grifly figure, who the ftern impell'd.
Wading behind, the horrid form appear'd ;   145
Above the water his ftrong arm he rear'd,
And crofs the creeping flood the crazy veffel fteer'd.
The heavenly Sprite obferv'd her trembling ward,
Whofe growing fears the hideous pafs abhorr'd,
And cheering thus fhe fpake : " This fpectre boafts
The chief dominion of thefe dreary coafts :   151
To him, thy pilot, without dread confign,
And place.thy body in his bark fupine !
So thro' this arching rock thou'lt pafs alone,
Safe from the perils of the incumbent ftone :   155
Embark undaunted !—on the farther fide
Thou'lt furely find me, thy unfailing guide.
Nor let this pilot raife thy groundlefs dread,
This fullen Charon of the froward dead,
A phantom, never bleft with human life,   160
Tho' oft on earth his noxious power is rife;
And in that region, ne'er from error free,
The words he dictates are affign'd to me.

I.   Obferve

Obferve this fiend, that Nature fcorn'd to frame,
Offspring of Pride, and Apathy his name!   165
Paffions he ne'er can feel, and ne'er impart,
A mifcreated imp, without a heart;
In place of which, his fubtle parent pinn'd
A bladder, fill'd with circulating wind,
Which feems with mimic life the mafs to warm, 170
And gives falfe vigour to his bloated form.
But place thee in the boat his arms direct,
My love fhall watch thee, and my power protect."

So fpake the friendly Sprite; th' obedient maid
Her form along the narrow veffel laid: 175
But oh! what terrors fhake her tender foul,
As from the fhore the bark begins to roll,
And, fever'd from her friend, her eyes difcern
The fteering fpectre wading at the ftern!
Far ftronger fears her refolution melt,   180
Than thofe, which erft the bard of Florence felt,
When, by the honour'd fhade of Virgil led
Thro' all the dreary circles of the dead,
Hell's fierceft demons threaten'd to divide
The living poet from his fhadowy guide;   185

And

And bade him, friendlefs, and alone, return,

Thro' the dire horrors of the dark fojourn.

Not long the lovely fair-one's terrors laft ;

For fafely thro' th' impending rock fhe paft :

And flow advancing to the gloomy ftrand,   190

The fullen pilot brings her fafe to land.

There, fondly hovering on her guardian plumes,

The heavenly Monitor her charge refumes ;

And fmiling, leads along the rocky road,

Whofe windings open into Spleen's abode.   195

   Thou queen of fhades ! whofe fpirit-damping fpell

Too oft is feen the poet's pride to quell,

May I, unpunifh'd by thy fubtle power,

Dare to difplay thy fubterranean bower,

And to this wond'ring upper world explain   200

The fhadowy horrors of thy fecret reign ?

   Entering beneath a wide fantaftic arch,

Round the drear circuit of the dome they march ;

Which a pale flafh from many a fiery fprite

Frequent illumes with intermitting light ;   205

Such, as on earth, to Superftition's eye,

Denounces ruin from the northern fky,

While

While fhe difcerns, amid the nightly glare,
Armies embattled in the blazing air.

Around the nymph unnumber'd phantoms glide ;
Here fwell the bloated race of bulky Pride :   211
In clofe and horrid union, there appear
The wilder progeny of frantic Fear ;
Mif-fhapen monfters ! whofe ftupendous frame
Abhorrent Nature has refus'd to name.   215
Here, in cameleon colours, lightly flit
The motley offspring of diforder'd Wit.
All things prodigious the wide cave contain'd,
And forms, beyond what fable ever feign'd :
But, as the worm, that on the dewy green   220
Springs half to view, and half remains ufeen,
Perceiving near its cell a human tread,
Slinks back to earth, and hides its timid head :
So, where the heavenly Spirit deign'd to lead,
The ftartled fpectres from her ftep recede ;   225
And, as abafh'd they from her eye retire,
Sink into mift, or melt in fluid fire.

High on an ebon throne, fuperbly wrought
With each fierce figure of fantaftic thought,

In

In a deep cove, where no bright beam intrudes, 230
O'er her black fchemes the fullen emprefs broods.
The fcreechowl's mingled with the raven's plume
Shed o'er her furrow'd brows an awful gloom;
A garb, that glares with ftripes of lurid flame,
Wraps in terrific pomp her haggard frame; 235
Round her a ferpent, as her zone, is roll'd,
Which, writhing, ftings itfelf in every fold.

Near her pavilion, in barbaric ftate,
Four mutes the mandates of their queen await.
From fickly Fancy bred, by fullen Sloth, 240
Both parents' curfe, yet pamper'd ftill by both,
Firft ftands Difeafe; an hag of magic power,
Varying her frightful vifage every hour,
Her horrors heightening, as thofe changes laft,
And each new form more hideous than the paft. 245
Detraction next, a fhapelefs fiend, appears,
Whofe fhrivell'd hand a mifty mirror rears;
Fram'd by malignant Art, th' infernal toy
Inverts the lovely mien of fmiling Joy,
Robs rofeate Beauty of attractive grace, 250
And gives a ftepdame's frown to Nature's face.

The

The third in place, but with a fiercer air,
See the true Gorgon Difappointment glare !
By whofe petrific power Delight's o'erthrown ;
And Hope's warm heart becomes an icy ftone.   255
Laft, in a gorgeous robe, that, ill beftow'd,
Bows her mean body by its cumbrous load,
Stands fretful Difcontent, of fiends the worft,
By dignity debas'd, by bleffings curft,
Who poifons Pleafure with the foureft leaven,   260
And makes a hell of Love's ecftatic heaven.

   The guide celeftial, near this ghaftly group,
Perceiv'd her tender charge with terror droop :
" Fear   not,   fweet   maid," fhe   cries,   " my   fteps
       purfue !
Nor gaze too long on this infernal crew !   265
Turn from Detraction's fafcinating glafs !
In filence crofs the throne ! obferve, and pafs !
Beyond this dome, the palace of the queen,
Her empire winds thro' many a dreary fcene,
Where fhe torments, as their deferts require,   270
Her various victims, that on earth expire ;
Each clafs apart : for in a different cell
The fierce, the fretful, and the fullen dwell :

                         Thefe

Thefe fhalt thou flightly view, in vapours hurl'd,
And fwiftly then regain thy native world.   275
But firft remark, within that ample nich,
With every quaint device of fplendor rich,
Yon phantom, who, from vulgar eyes withdrawn,
Appears to ftretch in one eternal yawn :
Of empire here he holds the tottering helm,   280
Prime minifter in Spleen's difcordant realm,
The pillar of her fpreading ftate, and more,
Her darling offspring, whom on earth fhe bore ;
For, as on earth his wayward mother ftray'd,
Grandeur, with eyes of fire, her form furvey'd,   285
And with ftrong paffion ftarting from his throne,
Unloos'd the fullen queen's reluctant zone.
From his embrace, conceiv'd in moody joy,
Rofe the round image of a bloated boy :
His nurfe was Indolence ; his tutor Pomp,   290
Who kept the child from every childifh romp ;
They rear'd their nurfling to the bulk you fee,
And his proud parents call'd their imp ENNUI.
This realm he rules, and in fuperb attire
Vifits each earthly palace of his fire :   295

A thoufand fhapes he wears, now pert, now prim,
Purfues each grave conceit, or idle whim;
In arms, in arts, in government engages,
With monarchs, poets, politicians, fages;
But drops each work, the moment it's begun,   300
And, trying all things, can accomplifh none:
Yet o'er each rank, and age, and fex, his fway
Spreads undifcern'd, and makes the world his prey.
The light coquet, amid flirtation, fighs,
To find him lurk in Pleafure's vain difguife;   305
And the grave nun difcovers, in her cell,
That holy water but augments his fpell.
As the ftrange monfter, of the ferpent breed,
That haunts, as travellers tell, the marfhy mead,
Devours each nobler beaft, tho' firmly grown   310
To fize and ftrength fuperior to his own;—
For on the grazing horfe, or larger bull,
Subtly he fprings, of dark faliva full,
With fwiftly-darting tongue his prey anoints
With venom, potent to diffolve its joints,   315
And, while its bulk in liquid poifon fwims,
Swallows its melting bone and fluid limbs:—

                                        So

So this Ennui, this wonder-working elf,
Can vanquiſh powers far mightier than himſelf:
Nor Wit nor Science ſoar his reach above,   320
And oft he ſeizes on ſucceſsful Love.
Of all the radiant hoſt who lend their aid
To light mankind thro' life's bewildering ſhade,
Bright Charity alone, with cloudleſs ray,
May boaſt exemption from his baleful ſway :   325
Haſte then, ſweet nymph, nor let us longer roam
Round the drear circle of this dangerous dome!
Leſt e'en thy guide, entangled in his ſpell,
Should fail to guard thee from a fiend ſo fell !"

　　So ſpeaking, the kind Spirit's anxious care   330
Led from the palace the attentive fair,
And, winding through a paſſage dark and rude,
Thus the mild monitor her ſpeech renew'd :
" 'Gainſt fear and pity now thy boſom ſteel,
For ſights more horrible I now reveal !   335
Spleen's tortur'd victims view with dauntleſs eyes ;
For lo ! her penal realms before thee riſe !"
The nymph advancing ſaw, with mute amaze,
A diſmal, deep, enormous dungeon blaze.

F 2

Stones

Stones of red fire the hideous wall compos'd;   340

And maffive gates the horrid confine clos'd,

Th' infernal portrefs of this doleful dome,

With fiery lips, that fwell'd with poifonous foam,

Pale Difcord, rag'd ; with whofe tormenting tongue,

Thro' all its caves th' extenfive region rung :   345

A living vulture was the fury's creft ;

And in her hand a rattlefnake fhe preft,

Whofe angry joints inceffantly were heard

To found defiance to the fcreaming bird.

  " The boundlefs depth of this dire prifon holds

The untam'd fpirits of imperious fcolds :   351

Nor think that females only fill the cave !

Male termagants have liv'd, and here they rave.

All of each fex are pent within this pale,

Who knew no ufe of language, but to rail."   355

Thus to her charge exclaim'd the heavenly guide,

And, as fhe fpoke, the portals open'd wide,

And to th' obfervance of the fhuddering maid,

Th' immeafurable den was all difplay'd.

But oh ! what various noifes from within   360

Fill the vext air with one ftupendous din !

                         Mourning's

Mourning's deep groan, and anger's furious call
Terror's loud cry, and affectation's squall,
The sob of paffion, the hyfteric fcream,
And fhrieks of frenzy, in its fierce extreme !   365
In this wild uproar every found's combin'd,
That ftuns the fenfes, and diftracts the mind.
" Mark" (to the nymph SOPHROSYNE began)
" The fierce Xantippe flaming in the van,
The vafe, fhe emptied on the fage's head,   370
Hangs o'er her own, a different fhower to fhed ;
For, drop by drop, diftilling liquid fire,
It fills the vixen with new tropes of ire.
  Beyond the Grecian dame extend your view,
And mark the fpectre of a modern fhrew !   375
She, who whene'er fhe din'd, with furious look,
Spurn'd her nice food, and bellow'd at her cook,
Here juftly feels a culinary rack,
Bound like Ixion, to a whirling jack."
SERENA gaz'd, but foon fhe turn'd away,   380
Mute with difguft, and fhuddering with difmay,
" To fcenes lefs hideous let us now repair !"
(Said the kind guard of the dejected fair)

And,

And, cheering her faint charge, her ſtep ſhe led
To the near dwelling of the fretful dead.   385
   Of duſky adamant the dungeon roſe ;
A dingy mirror its dark ſides compoſe,
Reflecting, with a thouſand quaint grimaces,
The pale inhabitants' diſtorted faces.
" Here, like a dame of quality array'd,   390
Sits Peeviſhneſs, preſiding o'er the ſhade,
And frowning at her own uncomely mien,
Whoſe coarſe reflection on the wall is ſeen.
A ſnarling lap-dog her right hand reſtrains,
Her lap an infant porcupine contains,   395
Which, while her fondneſs tries its wrath to ſtill,
Wounds her each moment with a pointed quill.
The froward ſpirits here in durance fret,
Whoſe teſty life was one continued pet ;
Here they in trifles that vexation find,   400
Which teaz'd on earth their irritated mind.
Obſerve the phantom, who with eyes aſkance
Still to the mirror turns her eager glance !
See ! to her cheek, inceſſant as ſhe turns,
Her vex'd blood ruſhes, and her viſage burns.   405

Beauty

Beauty for lafting blifs had form'd the maid ;
Love to her charms his faithful homage paid ;
But, all this fwelling tide of joy to check,
A fatal freckle rifes on her neck :
Her foft cofmetics the griev'd nymph applies,   410
Succefs attends her, and the freckle dies :
But ah ! this victory avails her not ;
She finds an hydra in the teazing fpot :
Faft as one flies, another ftill fucceeds,
And with eternal food her fretful humour feeds. 415
   Near to the nymph, in a more moody fit,
See the pale phantom of a peevifh wit !
Mark with what frowns his eager eyes perufe,
Wet from the prefs, three Critical Reviews !
With wounded vanity's diftracting rage ,   420
How rapidly he runs thro' every page !
He finds fome honours lavifh'd on his verfe,
And joy's faint gleams his gloomy fpirit pierce,
But oh ! too foon thefe feeble fparks decay :
And keen vexation reaffumes her prey.   425
Hating reproof, in every fibre fore,
One cenfur'd particle torments him more,

More

More than a hundred happier lines delight,
Which liberal favour condefcends to cite.

    But time will fail us, if we paufe to view   430
The various torments of the tefty crew;
Thefe wretched chymifts, whofe o'erheated brain
Extracts from nothing a fubftantial pain.
Yet, ere to different diftricts we advance,
Take of one fretful tribe a tranfient glance!   435
Their unfufpected punifhments fupply
A leffon, ufeful to the female eye.
Spleen's livelieft agent here beguiles the gay,
Fair to attract, and flattering to betray."
As thus the kind æthereal guardian fpoke,   440
Within a rock, whence plaintive murmurs broke,
She touch'd a fecret fpring, whofe power was fuch,
Two jarring doors unfolded at the touch,
And, with the charms of regal fplendor bright,
A chearful banquet fparkles to the fight.   445
Viands fo light, fo elegantly grac'd,
Might tempt e'en Temperance herfelf to tafte;
For fruits alone compos'd th' enticing treat,
Fair to the eye, and to the palate fweet.

                                In

In fuch bright juice the peach and cherry fwim, 450
As make the topaz and the ruby dim.
Here crown'd with every flower, and gaily dreft
In all the glitter of a Gallic veft,
Whofe ample folds her loathfome body fcreen'd,
A child of luxury reigns, a fubtle fiend ! 455
Who, with a grace that every heart allures,
Smiles on the luftre of her rich *liqueurs*.
Her fatal fmiles their utmoft power exert
To poifon beauty at her dire deffert ;
To blaft the rofe that health's bright cheek adorns,
And fill each feftive heart with latent thorns : 461
For the fly fiend, of every art poffeft,
Steals on th' affection of her female gueft ;
And, by her foft addrefs feducing each,
Eager fhe plies them with a brandy peach : 465
They with keen lip the lufcious fruit devour ;
But fwiftly feel its peace-deftroying power.
Quick thro' each vein new tides of frenzy roll :
All evil paffions kindle in the foul,
Drive from each feature every chearful grace, 470
And glare ferocious in the fallow face ;

The

The wounded nerves in furious conflict tear,
Then sink, in blank dejection and despair.
Effects more dire, thus tempting to deceive,
The apple wrought not in the soul of Eve; 475
Howe'er disguis'd, in jelly or in jam,
Spleen has no poison surer than a dram.

    " But haste we now" (the heavenly leader cries)
" To where this penal world's last wonder lies!"
She spoke; and led the nymph thro' deeper dells, 480
Low-murmuring vaults, and horror-breathing cells.
And now they pass a perforated cage,
Where rancorous spectres without number rage.
" Avert thine eye!" (the heavenly Spirit said)
" Nor view these abject tribes of envious dead! 485
Who pin'd to hear the voice of truth proclaim
A sister's beauty, or a brother's fame!
Tho' crown'd with all prosperity imparts,
High in their various ranks, and several arts;
Yet, meanly sunk by envy's base controul, 490
They died in that consumption of the soul;
And here, thro' bars that twisted adders make,
And the long volumes of th' envenom'd snake,

                        O'er

O'er this dark road they dart an anxious eye,
Still envying evey fiend that flutters by. 495
Pafs ! and regard them not !"—Th' attentive maid
In filent tremor the beheft obey'd.

This dungeon croft, her weary feet fhe drags
Thro' winding caverns, and o'er icy crags :
Soul-chilling damps in the dark paffage reign, 500
Which iffues on a vaft and dreary plain,
Fann'd by no breezes, with no verdure crown'd ;
The black horizon is its only bound.
And now advancing, in a drizzly mift,
Thro' fullen phantoms, hating to exift, 505
SERENA fpies, high o'er his fubjects plac'd,
The ghaftly tyrant of the gloomy wafte.
Murmuring he fits upon a rocking ftone,
Th' unftable bafe of his ill-founded throne :
Hideous his face, and horrible his frame, 510
Mifanthropy the grizly monfter's name !
Him to fierce Pride, with raging paffion fore,
The frowning gorgon, Difappointment, bore ;
On earth detefted, and by heaven abhorr'd,
Of this drear wild he reigns the moody lord. 515

9   Few

Few are the fubjects of his wafte domain,
And fcarce a female in his frightful train,
Except one changing corps of ancient prudes:
Reluctant here the prying band intrudes.
Each, who on earth, behind her artful fan,   520
Feign'd coarfe averfion to the creature man,
Is doom'd, in this dark region, to abide
Some tranfient pains for hypocritic pride.
Here ever-during chains thofe fcoffers bind,
Whofe writings deaden and debafe the mind; 525
Who mock creation with injurious fcorn,
And feel a fancied void in plenty's horn.

In his right-hand, an emblem of his cares,
A branch of aconite the monarch bears;
And thofe four phantoms, who this region haunt,
He feeds with berries from this deadly plant; 531
For, ftrange to tell! tho' fever'd from its root,
The bough ftill blackens with fucceffive fruit.
The tribes, who tafte it, burft into a fit
Of raving mockery and rancorous wit; 535
And, pleas'd their tyrant's ghaftly fmile to court,
By vile diftortions make him various fport.

The

The frantic rabble, who his fway confefs,
Before his throne an hideous puppet drefs ;
When in unfeemly rags they have array'd   540
The image, from their own dark femblance made,
In horrid gambols round their work they throng,
With antic dance and rude difcordant fong ;
Satire's rank offals on the block they fling,
And call it nature, to delight their king :   545
While in their features he exults to fee
The frowns of torture, mixt with grins of glee.
For, as thefe abject toils engage the crew,
Their own grim-idol darkens to their view ;
Wide and more wide its horrid ftature fpreads,   550
And o'er the tribe new confternation fheds :
For each forgets, in his bewilder'd gaze,
'Tis but a monfter, which he help'd to raife.
As o'er its form their dizzy glances roll,
It ftrikes a chearlefs damp thro' all the foul.   555
Vainly to fhun the baleful fight they try,
It draws for ever the reluctant eye :
At each review with deeper dread they ftart ;
A colder chaos numbs each freezing heart.

No

No mutual confidence, no friendly care,   560
Relieves the panic they are doom'd to bear;
For as they fhrink abforb'd in wild affright,
When each to each inclines his wounded fight.
They feel, for focial comfort, four difguft,
And all the fullen anguifh of diftruft.   565
    Around,thefe wretches in the drear abode,
The ghaftly grinning fiend Derifion rode,
Who to their wayward minds on earth fupplied
Perverted ridicule's malignant tide.
His fteed of Pegafus the femblance bore;   570
But with falfe wings, that knew not how to foar
Where'er he pafs'd, with mifchief in his look,
A founding whip of knotted fnakes he fhook;
And laugh'd in lafhing each pretended fage,
Whofe malice wore the mafk of moral rage.   575
An uncouth bugle his left-hand difplay'd,
From a grey monkey's fkull by Cunning made,
And form'd to pour, in harmony's defpite,
Sounds that each jarring fenfe of pain excite:
And now his livid lips this bugle blew;   580
Thro' every den the piercing difcord flew:

                                    The

The fiends all anfwer'd in one hideous yell,
And in a fearful trance SERENA fell.
Hence from the lovely nymph her fenfes fled,
Till, thro' the parted curtains of her bed, 585
The amorous fun, who now began to rife,
Kift, with a fportive beam, her opening eyes.

END OF THE THIRD CANTO.

CANTO

CANTO IV.

HAIL, thou enlighten'd globe of human joy!
Where focial cares the foften'd heart employ:
What cheering rays of vital comfort roll
In thy bright regions o'er the refcued foul,
Which, 'fcaping from the dark domain of Spleen, 5
Springs with new warmth to thy attractive fcene!
Once more I blefs thy pleafure-breathing gale,
And gaze enchanted on thy flowery vale,
Where fmiling innocence, and ardent youth,
Sport hand in hand with beauty and with truth. 10
Sport on, fweet revellers! in rofy bowers,
Safe from th' intrufion of all evil powers!
Ah fruitlefs wifh of the benignant Mufe,
Which to this chequer'd world the Fates refufe!
For round its precincts many an ugly fprite 15
Speeds undifcern'd to poifon pure delight:

Amidft

Amidſt the foremoſt of this haggard band,
Unwearied poſter of the ſea and land,
Wrapt in dark miſts, malignant Scandal flies,
While Envy's poiſon'd breath the buoyant gale ſup-
 plies: 20
Tho' SHERIDAN, with ſhafts of comic wit,
Pierc'd, and expos'd her to the laughing pit,
Th' immortal hag ſtill wears her paper crown,
The dreaded empreſs of the idle town :
O'erleaping her prerogative of old,   25
To ſink the noble, to defame the bold ;—
In chaſe of worth to ſlip the dogs of ſtrife,
Thro' all the ample range of public life ;—
The tyrant now, that ſanctuary burſt
Where happineſs by privacy is nurſt,   30
Her fury riſing as her powers increaſe,
O'erturns the altars of domeſtic peace.
Pleas'd in her dark and gall-diſtilling cloud
The ſportive form of innocence to ſhroud,
Beauty's young train her baleful eyes ſurvey,   35
To mark the faireſt, as her favourite prey.

 VOL. V.   G   Hence,

Hence, sweet SERENA, while thy spirit stray'd
Round the deep realms of subterranean shade,
This keenest agent of th' infernal powers
On earth was busied, in those tranquil hours,   40
To blast thy peace, and poison'd darts to aim
Against the honour of thy spotless name :
For Scandal, restless fiend, who never knows
The balmy blessing of an hour's repose,
Worn, yet unsated with her daily toil,   45
In her base work consumes the midnight oil.
O'er fiercer fiends when heavy slumbers creep,
When wearied avarice and ambition sleep,
Scandal is vigilant, and keen to spread
The plagues that spring from her prolific head.   50
On truth's fair basis she her falsehood builds,
With tinsel sentiment its surface gilds ;
To nightly labour from their dark abodes
The demons of the groaning press she goads,
And smiles to see their rapid art supply   55
Ten thousand wings to every infant lie.

    In triumph now behold the hag applaud
Her keen and fav'rite imp, ingenious Fraud,

Her

Her quick compofitor, whofe flying hand
Has clos'd the paragraph fhe keenly plann'd.   60
No nymph fhe nam'd, yet mark'd her vile intent,
That dulnefs could not mifs the name fhe meant:
In fatire's tints the injur'd fair fhe drew,
In form an angel, but in foul a Jew.

It chanc'd her fire among his friends inroll'd   65
A wealthy fenator, infirm and old;
Who, dup'd too early by a generous heart,
Rafhly affum'd a mifanthropic part:
Tho' peevifh fancies would his mind incruft,
Good-nature's image lurk'd beneath their ruft;   70
And gay SERENA, with that fportive wit
Which heals the folly that it deigns to hit,
Would oft the ficknefs of his foul beguile,
And teach the fullen humorift to fmile;
Pleas'd by her virtuous frolics to affuage   75
The mental anguifh of diftemper'd age.
This ancient friend, in a farcaftic fketch,
Was mark'd by Scandal as a monied wretch,
For whom the young, yet mercenary fair
Had fubtly fpread a matrimonial fnare.   80

With such base matter, more diffusely wrought,
The spirit-piercing paragraph was fraught,
O'er which with glee the eye of Scandal glar'd,
Which for the opening press herself prepar'd;
She on the types her inky wad let fall,   85
And smear'd each letter with her bitterest gall;
The press, whose ready gripe the charge receives,
Stamps it successive on ten thousand leaves,
Which pil'd in heaps impatient seem to lie,
They only wait the dawn of day to fly.   90
  Now, as the child, in lonely chamber laid,
Mute in the dark, and of itself afraid,
When, haply conscious of the pain it feels,
The watchful mother to its pillow steals,
Springs to her breast, and shakes off all alarms,   95
Feeling its safety in her fostering arms:
With such quick joy, in innocence as young,
The soft SERENA from her pillow sprung,
Pleas'd to awake from her terrific dream,
And feel the chearful's sun's returning beam.   100
Eager she rose, in busy thought, nor staid
The wonted summons of her punctual maid,

And

And as her own fair hands adjuſt her veſt,
The guardian cincture flutters on her breaſt;
For fondly, when ſhe wak'd, or when ſhe ſlept,   105
Still round her heart th' important zone ſhe kept.
Thou happy girdle! to thy charge be juſt!
Firm be thy threads, and faithful to their truſt;
For hours approach, when all the ſtores they hide
Of magic virtue, muſt be ſtrongly tried!—   110
Now, while her kind domeſtic heart intends
To pleaſe her early ſire, the nymph deſcends;
But ſleep, who left the fair with ſudden flight,
With late wings hover'd o'er the good old knight;
And the chill circle of the lone ſaloon   115
Informs the ſhiv'ring maid ſhe roſe too ſoon.
'Tis true, attentive John's unfailing care
Began the rites of breakfaſt to prepare;
But yet no fires on the cold altar burn,
No ſmoke ariſes from the ſilver urn,   120
And the blank tea-board, where no viands lay,
Only ſupplied the paper of the day.
   Tho' mild SERENA's peace-devoted mind
The keen debate of politics declin'd,

And

And heard with cold contempt, or generous hate, 125
The frauds of party and the lies of state ;
Nor car'd much more for fashion's loose intrigues,
Than factious bickerings or foreign leagues ;
Yet, while she saunters idle and alone,
Her careless eyes are on the paper thrown.   130

    As some gay youth, whom sportive friends engage
To view the furious ourang in his cage,
If while amus'd he sees the monster grin,
And trusts too careless to the bolts within,
If the sly beast, as near the grate he draws,   135
Tear him unguarded with projected paws,
Starts at the wound, and feels his bosom thrill
With pain and wonder at the sudden ill :
So did SERENA start, so wildly gaze,
In such mixt pangs of anguish and amaze,   140
Feeling the wound which Scandal had design'd
To lacerate her mild and modest mind.
Startled, as one who from electric wire
Unheeding catches unsuspected fire,
She reads, then almost doubts that she has read,   145
And thinks some vision hovers round her head.

                             Now,

Now, her fixt eye fome ftriking words confine,
And now fhe darts it thrice thro' every line;
Nor could amazement more her fenfes fhake,
Had every letter been a gorgon's fnake.   150
Now rifing indignation takes its turn,
And her flufh'd cheeks with tingling blufhes burn,
With reftlefs motion and with many a frown,
Thro' the wide room fhe paces up and down:
Now, mufing, makes a momentary ftand,   155
The fatal paper fluttering in her hand.
So the fhy bird, by cruel fportfmen fprung,
And by their random fire feverely ftung,
Scar'd, not difabled, by the diftant wound,
Now trembling flies, now fkims along the ground, 160
Now vainly tries, in fome fequefter'd fpot,
From her gor'd breaft to fhake the galling fhot.
   Ye tender nymphs ! whofe kindling fouls would
     flame,
Touch'd, like SERENA's, by injurious blame,
O let your quick and kindred fpirits form   165
A vivid picture of the mental ftorm

In

In which she labour'd, and whose force to paint
The Muse's strongest tints appear too faint;
In sympathetic thought her suffering see!
But O, for ever from such wrongs be free!   170

Her faithful girdle try'd its power to save,
And oft a monitory impulse gave;
Still unregarded, still unfelt, it prest
With useless energy her heaving breast,
Her mind, forgetful of the magic zone,   175
Full of the burning shaft by Scandal thrown,
With blended notes of sorrow and disdain,
Thus in disorder'd language vents its pain:——
" Had malice dar'd my honour to defame,
The self-refuted lie had lost its aim: 180
But here the world, deceiv'd by sland'rous art,
Must think SERENA has a venal heart."
A venal heart! at that detested sound,
In swelling anguish her sunk voice was drown'd.
Now was a fearful crisis of her fate: 185
Distended now by passion's growing weight,
And for its mistress fill'd with conscious dread,
The magic girdle crack'd thro' every thread,

                                        And

And ſnapp'd perchance by Scandal's force accurſt,
From her full heart the guardian zone had burſt, 190
And, ſpite of all the virtues of the fair,
The ſpell of happineſs had ſunk in air,
But that SOPHROSYNE, whoſe friendly fear
Timely foreſaw this trial too ſevere,
An early ſuccour gain'd from ſecret love,   195
From the fell kite to ſnatch the falling dove.

 As Nature ſtudies, in her wide domain,
To blend ſome antidote with every bane ;
Thus her kind aid the friendly power contriv'd, 199
That, from the quarter whence the wound arriv'd,
There flow'd, the anguiſh of that wound to calm,
A ſoothing, ſoft, and medicinal balm.
As in her agitated hand the fair
Wav'd the looſe paper with diſorder'd air,
In capitals ſhe ſaw SERENA flame :   205
She bluſh'd, ſhe ſhudder'd, as ſhe view'd the name;
Her ready fears ſubſide in new ſurpriſe,
And eager thus ſhe reads with lighten'd eyes :

            " Go,

" Go, faithful fonnet, to SERENA fay   209
    What charms peculiar in her features reign.:
A ftranger, whom her glance may ne'er furvey,
    Pays her this tribute in no flattering ftrain.
Tell her, the bard, in beauty's wide domain,
    Has feen a virgin cheek as richly glow,
A bofom, where the blue meandring vein   215
    Sheds as foft luftre thro' the lucid fnow,
Eyes, that as brightly flafh with joy and youth,
    And locks, that like her own luxuriant flow:
Then fay, for then fhe cannot doubt thy truth,
    That the wide earth no female form can fhow
Where nature's legend fo diftinctly tells,   221
    In this fair fhrine a fairer fpirit dwells."

With curious wonder the reviving maid
View'd this fond homage to her beauty paid;
A fecond glance o'er every line fhe caft,   225
And half pronounc'd and half fupprefs'd the laft,
While modeft pleafure, and ingenuous pride,
Her burning cheek with deeper crimfon dy'd.
                                        *   O Praife !

O Praife ! thy language was by heaven defign'd
As manna to the faint bewilder'd mind :   230
Beauty and diffidence, whofe hearts rejoice
In the kind comfort of thy cheering voice,
In this wild wood of life, wert thou not nigh,
Muft, like the wandering babes, lie down and die :
But thy fweet accents wake new vital powers,   235
And make this thorny path a path of flowers :
As oil on ocean's troubled waters fpread,
Smooths the rough billow to a level bed,
The foothing rhyme thus foften'd into reft
The painful tumult of SERENA's breaft.   240

  Now, to herfelf reftor'd, the confcious maid
The lurking fiend's infidious fnare furvey'd ;
Her nerves, with grateful trepidation, own
A flighter preffure from the faithful zone ;
And in fond thought fhe breathes a thankful prayer
For her ætherial guardian's conftant care ;   246
Yet with a keen defire her bofom glow'd,
To hear from whom the gentle fonnet flow'd ;
But kind SOPHROSYNE, who watch'd unfeen,
To fhield her votary from the wiles of Spleen,   250
           As

As friendly love had fixt a future time,
When to reveal the fecret of the rhyme,
Strove till that hour her fancy to reftrain,
Nor let her anxious wifhes rife to pain.

 As gaiety's frefh tide began to roll,   255
Faft in the fwelling channel of her foul,
The good old knight defcends, tho' eager, flow,
The gout ftill tingling in his tender toe ;
And now, paternal falutations paft,
His eyes he keenly on the paper caft,   260
While his fweet daughter, with attentive grace,
Before him flies his ready cup to place ;
For tea and politics alternate fhare,
In friendly rivalfhip, his morning care.
Tho' fmooth as oil the knight's good-humour flows,
When the mild breeze of pleafant fortune blows, 266
Yet, quick to catch the cafual fparks of ire,
Like oil it kindles into mounting fire ;
And fiercely now his flaming fpirit blaz'd,
While on thofe galling words he wildly gaz'd,   270
Whofe force had almoft work'd into a ftorm
The gentler elements in beauty's form.

           As

As the farcaſtic ſentence caught his view,
Back from the board his elbow-chair he drew,
And, by ſharp ſtings of ſudden fury prick'd,   275
Far from his foot his gouty ſtool he kick'd.
Fierce as Achilles, by Atrides ſtung,
He pour'd the ſtream of vengeance from his tongue ;
But ah, thoſe angry threats he deign'd to ſpeak,
Had ſounds, alas ! far differing from the Greek. 280
Rage from his lips in legal language broke ;
Of juries and of damages he ſpoke,
And on the printer's law-devoted head
He threaten'd deep revenge in terms moſt dread ;
Terms, that with pain the ear of beauty pierce, 285
And oaths too rough to harmonize in verſe.

    While thus the good old knight, with paſſion hot,
His toaſt neglected, and his tea forgot,
The diſcord of the drama to increaſe,
Now prim PENELOPE aſſails her niece ;   290
For, as SIR GILBERT now, with choler dumb,
Points her the period with his angry thumb,
" Ah ! brother," cries the ſtiff, malignant crone,
(Her ſharp eye ſwiftly thro' the ſentence thrown)
                              " Scandal

" Scandal could never rife to heights like this,   295
But from the manners of each modern mifs ;
Had but my niece, lefs giddy and more grave,
Obferv'd the prudent hints I often gave———"
    The honeft knight her vile conclufion faw,
And quick curtail'd it with a tefty " Pfhaw !"   300
Mean while the gentle maid, who heard the taunt,
Survey'd without a frown her prudifh aunt :
Far other thoughts employ'd her fofter mind,
To one fweet purpofe all her foul inclin'd ;
How fhe might clofe th' unpleafant fcene, how beft
Reftore good humour to her father's breaft.   306
Her airy guardian with delight furvey'd
Thefe tender wifhes in the lovely maid,
And, to accomplifh what her heart defir'd,
Trains of new thought above her age infpir'd.   310
    As Venus on her fon's enlighten'd face
Shed richer charms, and more attractive grace;
When, iffuing forth from the diffolving cloud,
His bright form burft on the admiring crowd :
So kind SOPHROSYNE, unfeen, fupplies   315
A livelier radiance to SERENA's eyes ;

                                    And,

And, ere she speaks, to captivate her sire,
Touches her lips with patriotic fire.

   It chanc'd, that, toss'd upon a vacant chair,
A volume of that wit lay near the fair,   320.
Whose value, try'd by fashion's varying touch,
Once rose too high, and now is sunk too much;
The book, which fortune plac'd within her reach,
Contain'd, O CHESTERFIELD, the liberal speech
In which thy spirit, like an Attic sage,   325
Strove to defend the violated stage
From fetters basely forg'd by ministerial rage.
From this the nymph her useful lesson took,
And thus began, reclining on the book :—
" If on this noble lord we may rely,   330
Scandal is but a speck on Freedom's eye ;
And public spirit, then, will rather bear
The casual pain it gives by growing there,
Than, by a rash attempt to move it thence,
Hazard the safety of a precious sense,   335
And, by the efforts of a vain desire,
Rob this life-darting eye of all its fire.

                            Tho,

Tho' the foft breaft of innocence may fmart,
By cruel calumny's corroding dart,
Yet would fhe rather ache in every nerve,   340
And bear thofe pangs fhe knows not to deferve,
Much rather than be made a fenfelefs tool,
To aid the frenzy of tyrannic rule,
Or forge one dangerous bolt for power to aim
At facred Liberty's fuperior frame."——   345
 As ancient chiefs were wont of old to gaze,
With eyes of tender awe and fond amaze
On the fair prieftefs of the Delphic fane,
When firft fhe utter'd her prophetic ftrain,   349
Entranc'd in wonder, thus SIR GILBERT view'd
His child, yet more infpir'd, who thus purfu'd :
" For me, I own, thefe lines, with gall replete,
Shot thro' my fimple heart a fudden heat ;
But happier thoughts my rifing rage repreft,
And turn'd the pointlefs infult to a jeft :   355
And O ! fhould Slander ftill new wrath awake,
Still may my father, for his daughter's fake,
Difdain the vengeance of litigious ftrife,
And let SERENA's anfwer be—her life !"

She

She ended with a smile, whose magic flame   360
Shot youthful vigour thro' her father's frame :
His age, his anger, and his gout, are fled ;
" Enchanting girl !" with tears of joy, he said,
" Enchanting girl !" twice echoed from his tongue,
As, speaking, from his elbow-chair he sprung,   365
" Come to thy father's arms !—By Heaven, thou art
His own true offspring, and a Whig in heart."

He spoke ; and his fond arms around her curl'd
With proud grasp, seeming to infold the world.
Her conscious heart she feels with triumph beat, 370
And joys to find that triumph is compleat ;
For stiff PENELOPE, who near them stood,
" Albeit unused to the melting mood,"
Squeez'd from her eye-lid one reluctant tear,
And soften'd with a smile her brow severe ;   375
But 'twas a smile of such a gloomy grace,
As lighten'd once upon Alecto's face,
When Orpheus past her, leading back to life,
From Pluto's regions, his recover'd wife,
When love connubial, join'd to music's spell,   380
Moisten'd with tender joy the eyes of hell.

VOL. V.   H   Far

Far other smiles, with pleasure's softest air,
Gild the gay features of the youthful fair:
She looks like sportive Spring, when her young
  charms
Wind round her hoary sire's reluctant arms,   385
And, by a frolic infantine embrace,
Banish the rugged frown from Winter's face.
 Thro' the long day she felt the glowing tide
Of exultation thro' her bosom glide;
And oft she wish'd for slow-approaching night,   390
To hold sweet converse with her guardian sprite.
At length the hour approach'd her heart desir'd,
And, in her lonely chamber now retir'd,
Her tender fancy gave the fondest scope
To ardent gratitude and eager hope.   395
" Dear airy being !" (the soft nymph exclaim'd)
" Whose power can break the spell that Spleen has
  fram'd,
Can, by the waving of thy viewless wing,
O'er darkest forms a golden radiance fling,
And make, in minds by sorriest thoughts perplext, 400
This moment's grief the triumph of the next;

I bless

I blefs thy fuccour in each trial paſt ;
Be preſent ſtill, and ſave me in the laſt !"
   Thus, with her lovely eyes devoutly fixt,
Where rays of hope, and fear, and reverence mixt,
The tender fair her faithful guard addreſt,   406
Then with her cheek her downy pillow preſt ;
But long her wakeful lids refuſe to cloſe,
For curioſity diſpels repoſe.
Her buſy mind the myſtic veil would pierce,   410
That hides the author of the pleaſing verſe ;
Her lips involuntary catch the chime,
And half articulate the ſoothing rhyme,
Till weary thought no longer watch can keep,
But ſinks reluctant in the folds of ſleep.   415

END OF THE FOURTH CANTO.

H 2   CANTO

CANTO V.

WHY art thou fled, O bleſt poetic time,
　　When Fancy wrought the miracles of rhyme;
When, darting from her ſtar-encircled throne,
Her poet's eye commanded worlds unknown;
When, by her fiat made a mimic god,　　　　　5
He ſaw exiſtence waiting on his nod,
And at his pleaſure into being brought
New ſhadowy hoſts, the vaſſals of his thought,
In joy's gay garb, in terror's dread array,
Darker than night, and brighter than the day;　　10
Who, at his bidding, thro' the wilds of air,
Rais'd willing mortals far from earthly care,
And led them wondering thro' his wide domain,
Beyond the bounds of nature's narrow reign;
While their rapt ſpirits, in the various flight,　　15
Shook with ſuceſſive thrills of new delight?

Return,

Return, fweet feafon, grac'd with fiction's flowers,

Let not cold fyftem cramp thy genial powers!

Shall mild Morality, in garb uncouth,

The houfewife garb of plain and homely truth,   20

Robb'd by ftern Method of her rofy crown,

Chill her faint votaries by a wintry frown?

No; thou fweet friend of man, as fuits thee beft,

Shine forth in Fable's rich-embroider'd veft!

O make my verfe thy vehicle, thy arms,   25

To fpread o'er focial life thy potent charms!

And thou, SOPHROSYNE, myfterious fprite!

If haply I may trace thy fteps aright,

Roving thro' paths untrod by mortal feet,

To paint for human eyes thy heavenly feat,   30

Shed on my foul fome portion of that power,

Which fav'd SERENA in the trying hour,

To bear thofe trials, which, however hard,

As bards all tell us, may befall the bard;

The fop's pert jeft, the critic's frown fevere,   35

Learning's proud cant, with envy's artful fneer,

And, the vext poet's laft and worft difgrace,

His cold blank bookfeller's rhyme-freezing face.

Hence!

Hence ! ye dark omens, that to Spleen belong,
Ye fhall not check the current of my fong, 40
While Beauty's lovely race, for whom I fing,
Fire my warm hand to ftrike the ready ftring.

 As quiet now her lighteft mantle laid
O'er the ftill fenfes of the fleeping maid,
Her nightly vifitant, her faithful guide, 45.
Defcends in all her empyrean pride ;
That fairy fhape no more fhe deigns to wear,
Whofe light foot fmooths the furrow plough'd by care
In mortal faces, while her tiny fpear
Gives a kind tingle to the caution'd ear. 50
Now, in her nobler fhape, of heavenly fize,
She ftrikes her votary's foul with new furprife.
Jove's favourite daughter, arm'd in all his powers,
Appear'd lefs brilliant to th' attending Hours,
When, on the golden car of Juno rais'd, 55
In heavenly pomp the queen of battles blaz'd :
With all her luftre, but without the dread
Which from her arm the frowning gorgon fhed,
Sophrosyne defcends, with guardian love,
To waft her gentle ward to worlds above. 60

        From

From her fair brow a radiant diadem
Rofe in twelve ftars, and every feparate gem
Shot magic rays, of virtue to controul
Some paffion hoftile to the human foul.
Round her fweet form a robe of æther flow'd,   65
And in a wonderous car the fmiling Spirit rode;
Firm as pure ivory, it charm'd the fight
With finer polifh and a fofter white.
The hand of beauty, with an eafy fwell,
Scoop'd the free concave like a bending fhell;   70
And on its rich exterior, art difplay'd
The triumphs of the Power the car convey'd.
Here, in celeftial tints, furpaffing life,
Sate lovely Gentlenefs, difarming Strife;
There, young Affection, born of tender Thought,   75
In rofy chains the fiercer paffions caught;
Ambition, with his fceptre fnapt in twain,
And Avarice, fcorning what his chefts contain.
Round the tame vulture flies the fearlefs dove;
Soft Innocence embraces playful Love;   80
And laughing Sport, the frolic child of Air,
Buries in flowers the finking form of Care.

H 4

Thefe figures, pencil'd with a touch fo light,
That every image feem'd an heavenly fprite,
Breathe on the car; whofe fight-enchanting frame 85
Four wheels fuftain, of pale and purple flame;
For no fleet animals, to earth unknown,
Bear thro' ætherial fields this flying throne.
As by the fubtle electrician's fkill,
Globes feem to fly, obedient to his will;   90
So thefe four circles of inftinctive fire
Move by the impulfe of their queen's defire.
Mount or defcend by her directing care,
Or reft, fupported by the buoyant air.

Now, fpringing from her car, that hovering ftaid
High in the chamber of the fleeping maid,   96
The goddefs, with a voice divinely clear,
Breath'd thefe kind accents in her votary's ear:—
" Come, my fair champion, who fo well haft fought
The ufeful battles of contentious thought;   100
To aid thy gentle fpirit to fuftain
The final conflict of thy deftin'd pain,
View the rewards that, in my realms of blifs,
Wait the fweet victor in fuch war as this !

So

So haply may thy mind, with ſtrength renew'd,   105
The dark devices of the fiend elude;
By one bleſt effort ſeal thy triumphs paſt,
And gain thy promis'd guerdon in the laſt."
    As thus ſhe ſpake, her heavenly arms embrac'd,
And in the car the conſcious maiden plac'd,   110
Quick at her wiſh the flaming wheels aſcend,
No clouds impede them, whereſoe'er they bend,
As thro' the empire of the winds they ruſh'd,
The winds were all in mute ſubmiſſion huſh'd:
And now SERENA, from th' exalted car,   115
Look'd down, aſtoniſh'd, on each ſinking ſtar;
Flying o'er lucid orbs, whoſe diſtant light
Yet has not reach'd the ſcope of human ſight;
And now, not diſtant from the bounds of ſpace,
The guardian ſprite ſuſpends their rapid race;   120
And, while in deep amaze the nymph admires
The circling meteors' inoffenſive fires,
Pleas'd at her wonder, the mild Power addreſt,
With kind intelligence, her earthly gueſt:—
" Of thoſe three orbs, that in yon cryſtal ſphere   125
A ſeparate ſyſtem in themſelves appear,

                                        The

The laſt, whoſe luminous and ſteady form
Shines ſoftly bright, and moderately warm,
Contains my palace, and the gentle train
Whom I have wafted to this pure domain.   130
At equal diſtance my dominions lie
From theſe two larger worlds, more near thine eye :
Obſerve their difference as our wheels advance,
And paſſing, take of each a tranſient glance."

  So ſpeaking, to the groſſer globe ſhe ſprung,   135
Her car ſuſpended o'er its ſurface hung,
In heavy air ; for round this orb was roll'd
A circling vapour, dull, and damp, and cold.
" Here," ſays SOPHROSYNE, " thoſe beings dwell,
Who wanted ſoul to act or ill or well ;   140
Who ſaunter'd thoughtleſs thro' their mortal time,
Without a care, a virtue, or a crime ;
Here ſtill they ſaunter, in this languid ſcene :
But paſs the dozing crowd, and mark their queen."
And now, ſlow riding on a tortoiſe' back,   145
Her features lifeleſs, and each fibre ſlack,
Full in their view the nymph Indifference came ;
The quick SERENA ſoon perceiv'd her name ;

                         For,

For, as in folemn creeping ftate fhe rode,
In her lax hand fhe held fair GREVILLE's ode.   150
Ne'er did the mufe from her fweet treafure cull
Incenfe fo precious for a Power fo dull.
Still as fhe mov'd along her even way,
The heavy goddefs try'd to read the lay ;
But at each paufe her inattentive eye   155
Stray'd from the paper, which fhe held awry ;
Nor could her lips a fingle line repeat,
Tho' the foft verfe, moft ravifhingly fweet,
Thro' Time's juft ear will lafting pleafure fpread,
And charm the poppy from Oblivion's head.   160
Thus, like a city mayor, whofe heavy barge
Steers its dull progrefs at the public charge,
This Power, fo cumber'd by her empire's weight,
Makes her flow circuit round her fluggifh ftate.
Around her, tribes of rambling fceptics crawl,   165
Tho' moving, dubious if they move at all.
Before her, languid Pomp, her marfhal, creeps,
Whofe hand her banner half unfolded keeps :
Its quaint device her dull dominion fpoke—
An eagle, numb'd by the torpedo's ftroke.   170

                         " Enough

"Enough of scenes so foreign to thy soul,"
SOPHROSYNE exclaim'd; "from this dark goal
Pass we to regions opposite to this."
She spoke; and, darting o'er the wide abyss,
Her car, like lightning in soft flashes hurl'd,   175
Shot to the confines of a clearer world.
Now lovelier views the virgin's mind absorb;
For now they hover'd o'er a lucid orb.
Here the soft air, luxuriantly warm,
Imparts new lustre to SERENA's form: 180
Her eyes with more expressive radiance speak,
And richer roses open on her cheek.
Here, as she gaz'd, she felt in every vein
A blended thrill of pleasure and of pain;
Yet every object glittering in her view,   185
Her quick regard with soft attraction drew.
SOPHROSYNE, who saw the gentle fair
Lean o'er these confines with peculiar care,
Smil'd at the tender interest she display'd,
And spoke regardful of the pensive maid: 190
"Well may'st thou bend o'er this congenial sphere;
For Sensibility is sovereign here.

                                        Thou

Thou feeft her train of fprightly damfels fport,
Where the foft fpirit holds her rural court ;
But fix thine eye attentive to the plain,   195
And mark the varying wonders of her reign."
As thus fhe fpoke, fhe pois'd her airy feat
High o'er a plain exhaling every fweet ;
For round its precincts all the flowers that bloom
Fill'd the delicious air with rich perfume ;   200
And in the midft a verdant throne appear'd,
In fimpleft form by graceful fancy rear'd,
And deck'd with flowers ; not fuch whofe flaunting
         dyes
Strike with the ftrongeft tint our dazzled eyes ;
But thofe wild herbs that tendereft fibres bear,   205
And fhun th' approaches of a damper air.
Here ftood the lovely ruler of the fcene,
And beauty, more than pomp, announc'd the queen.
The bending fnow-drop, and the briar-rofe,
The fimple circle of her crown compofe ;   210
Rofes of every hue her robe adorn,
Except th' infipid rofe without a thorn.
Thro' her thin veft her heighten'd beauties fhine ;
For earthly gauze was never half fo fine.

Of

Of that enchanting age her figure feems,   ·   215
When fmiling nature with the vital beams
Of vivid youth, and pleafure's purple flame,
Gilds her accomplifh'd work, the female frame,
With rich luxuriance tender, fweetly wild,
And juft between the woman and the child.   220
Her fair left arm around a vafe fhe flings,
From which the tender plant mimofa fprings :
Towards its leaves, o'er which fhe fondly bends,
The youthful fair her vacant hand extends
With gentle motion, anxious to furvey   225
How far the feeling fibres own her fway :
The leaves, as confcious of their queen's command,
Succeffive fall at her approaching hand ;
While her foft breaft with pity feems to pant,
And fhrinks at every fhrinking of the plant.   230
    Around their fovereign, on the verdant ground,
Sweet airy forms in myftic meafures bound.
The mighty mafter of the revel, Love,
In notes more foothing than his mother's dove,
Prompts the foft ftrain that melting virgins fing, 235
Or fportive trips around the frolic ring,

                                        Coupling,

Coupling, with radiant wreaths of lambent fire,
Fair fluttering Hope and rapturous Defire.
Unnumber'd damfels different charms difplay,
Penfive with blifs, or in their pleafures gay ; 240
And the wide profpect yields one touching fight
Of tender, yet diverfified delight.
But, the bright triumphs of their joy to check,
In the clear air there hangs a dufky fpeck ;
It fwells—it fpreads—and rapid, as it grows, 245
O'er the gay fcene a chilling fhadow throws.
The foft SERENA, who beheld its flight,
Sufpects no evil from a cloud fo light ;
For harmlefs round her the thin vapours wreath,
Not hiding from her view the fcene beneath ; 250
But ah ! too foon, with pity's tender pain,
She faw its dire effect o'er all the plain :
Sudden from thence the founds of anguifh flow,
And joy's fweet carols end in fhrieks of woe :
The wither'd flowers are fall'n, that bloom'd fo fair,
And poifon all the peftilential air. 256
From the rent earth dark demons force their way,
And make the fportive revellers their prey.

         Here

Here gloomy Terror, with a ſhadowy rope,
Seems, like a Turkiſh mute, to ſtrangle Hope ; 260
There jealous Fury drowns in blood the fire
That ſparkled in the eye of young Deſire ;
And lifeleſs Love lets mercileſs Deſpair
From his cruſh'd frame his bleeding pinions tear.
But pangs more cruel, more intenſely keen, 265
Wound and diſtract their ſympathetic queen :
With fruitleſs tears ſhe o'er their miſery bends ;
From her ſweet brow the thorny roſe ſhe rends,
And, bow'd by grief's inſufferable weight,
Frantic ſhe curſes her immortal ſtate : 270
The ſoft SERENA, as this curſe ſhe hears,
Feels her bright eye ſuffus'd with kindred tears ;
And her kind breaſt, where quick compaſſion ſwell'd,
Shar'd in each bitter ſuffering ſhe beheld.

  The guardian Power ſurvey'd her lovely grief, 275
And ſpoke in gentle terms of mild relief :
" For this ſoft tribe thy heavieſt fear diſmiſs,
And know their pains are tranſient as their bliſs :
Rapture and agony, in nature's loom,
Have form'd the changing tiſſue of their doom ; 280

Both

Both interwoven with fo nice an art,
No power can tear the twifted threads apart :
Yet happier thefe, to Nature's heart more dear,
Than the dull offspring in the torpid fphere,
Where her warm wifhes, and affections kind, 285
Lofe their bright current in the ftagnant mind.
Here grief and joy fo fuddenly unite,
That anguifh ferves to fublimate delight."

    She fpoke ; and, ere SERENA could reply,
The vapour vanifh'd from the lucid fky ; 290
The nymphs revive, the fhadowy fiends are fled,
The new-born flowers a richer fragrance fhed ;
The gentle ruler of the changeful land,
Smiling, refum'd her fymbol of command ;
Replac'd the rofes of her regal wreath, 295
Still trembling at the thorns that lurk beneath :
But, to her wounded fubjects quick to pay
The tender duties of imperial fway,
Their wants fhe fuccour'd, they her wifh obey'd,
And all recover'd, by alternate aid ; 300

While,

While, on the lovely queen's enchanting face,
Departed forrow's faint and fainter trace,
Gave to each touching charm a more attractive
    grace.
Now, laughing Sport, from the enlighten'd plain,
Clear'd with quick foot the veſtiges of pain ;   305
The gay ſcene grows more beautifully bright,
Than when it firſt allur'd SERENA's ſight,
Still her fond eyes o'er all the proſpect range,
Flaſhing ſweet pleaſure at the bliſsful change :
Her curious thoughts with fond attachment burn, 310
Yet more of this engaging land to learn.
She finds the chief attendants of the queen,
Sweet females, wafted from our human ſcene ;
But, as it chanc'd, while all the realm reviv'd,
A ſpirit maſculine from earth arriv'd :   315
Two airy guides conduct the gentle ſhade ;
Genius, in robes of braided flames array'd,
And a fantaſtic nymph, in manners nice,
Profuſely deck'd with many an odd device ;

                              Siſter

Sister of him, whose luminous attire   320
Flashes with unextinguishable fire ;
Like him in features, in her look as wild,
And Singularity by mortals styl'd.
The eager queen, and all her smiling court,
Surround the welcome shade in gentle sport ;   325
For in their new associate all rejoice,
All pant to hear the accents of his voice.
Tho' o'er his frame th' Armenian robe was flung,
The pleasing stranger spoke the Gallic tongue ;
But in that language his enchanting art   330
Inspir'd new energy, that seiz'd the heart ;
In terms so eloquent, so sweetly bold,
A story of disastrous love he told,
Convuls'd with sympathy, the list'ning train,
At every pause, with dear delicious pain,   335
Intreat him to renew the fascinating strain.
And now SERENA, with suspended breath,
Listen'd, and caught the tale of Julia's death ;
And quick she cries, ere tears had time to flow,
" Blest be this hour ! for now I see Rousseau." 340

         Fondly

Fondly fhe gaz'd, till the enchanting found
In fuch a potent fpell her fpirit bound,
That, loft in fweet illufion, fhe forgot
The promis'd fcenes of the fublimer fpot;
Till now her mild remembrancer, whofe care   345
Stray'd not a moment from the mortal fair,
Rous'd her rapt mind, preparing her to meet
The brighter wonders of her blifsful feat;
While her inftinctive car's obedient frame
Now upward rofe, like undulating flame.   350

    As when fome victor on the watery world,
Bright honour gilding all his fails unfurl'd,
Steers into port, while to the laughing fky
His ftreamers tell his triumph as they fly;
Expecting thoufands line the crowded ftrand,   355
Swell the glad voice, or wave the joyous hand,
Preffing to view the fight their vows implor'd,
And hail their glory and their ftrength reftor'd:
So the bleft beings of this fmiling fcene
Flock'd round the car of their returning queen.   360
The radiant car, from which they now alight,
Careful fhe gives to a felected fprite,

                                        A nymph

A nymph of fnowy veft and lovely frame,
Fidelity her fair and fpotlefs name;
Then, happy to review her hallow'd home, 365
Leads her fweet gueft to her celeftial dome.

Gentleft of powers! for every purpofe fit,
To ftrengthen wifdom, and embellifh wit;—
Thou, whofe foft arts, poffefs'd by thee alone,
Can give to virtue's voice a fweeter tone; 370
Allay the froft of age, or fire of youth,
And lend attraction to fevereft truth;
Improve e'en beauty by thy graceful eafe,
Or teach deformity herfelf to pleafe;—
Infpire the bard, whofe juft ambition pants 375
To guide weak mortals to thy heavenly haunts!
Grant him, in notes that, like thy foft controul,
Allure attention, and poffefs the foul;
Grant him to fhow, in luminous difplay,
The myftic wonders of thy fecret fway! 380

Now, at the fight of the prefiding power,
Wide fpread the gates of a ftupendous tower,
On whofe firm height, commanding nature's bound,
The faithful warder of the fort they found,

I 3   Wakeful

Wakeful Intelligence, a trufty fprite,   385
Whofe eyes are piercing as the folar light,
And ever on the watch to found alarm,
If aught of dufky hue, portending harm,
Should, in defiance of her mandate, dare
Approach the palace of th' imperial fair.   390
Within his ward, magnificently great,
Lies the rich armoury that guards her ftate.
Here ftands Conviction's ftrong and lucid fpear,
Whofe touch annihilates fufpenfe and fear;
Here, Truth's unfullied adamantine fhield,   395
Which, fave SOPHROSYNE, no power can wield;
And Reafon's trenchant blade of blazing fteel,
Its edge and polifh form'd by friendly zeal;
And, not lefs fure their deftin'd mark to hit,
Pointed by virtue's hand, the fhafts of Wit;   400
And Ridicule's ftrong bolt, whofe ftunning blow
Lays towering vice and fearlefs folly low.
Here too the goddefs kept, in myftic ftate,
Thofe fweet rewards that on her champions wait,
Guerdons more precious than triumphant palms:—
The glance of gratitude for mental alms,   406

Peace's

Peace's foft kifs, and reconcilement's tear,
And fmiles of fympathy, are treafur'd here.

Thefe precin_ts paft, now hand in hand they came
To the rich fabric of majeftic frame; 410
Inftinct with joy their fovereign to behold,
The gates of maffive adamant unfold;
And, as the gently-moving valves unclofe,
Myfterious mufic from their motion flows;
The airy notes thro' all the palace roam, 415
And dulcet echoes fill the feftive dome:
A gorgeous hall amaz'd SERENA's eyes,
Compar'd to which, in fplendor, ftrength, and fize,
The nobleft works of which tradition fings,
Judaic fhrine, or feat of Memphian kings, 420
Would feem more humble than the waxen cell
In which the fkilful bee is proud to dwell.
Here fits a power, in whofe angelic face
Beauty is fweeten'd by maternal grace;
Her radiant feat, furpaffing mortal art, 425
Supports an emblem of her liberal heart,
A pelican, who rears her callow brood,
And from her vitals feems to draw their food.

I 4   Around

Around this fpirit flock a filial hoft,

Who blefs her empire, and her guidance boaft.　430

Here every fcience, all the arts attend,

In her they hail their parent and their friend ;

Each to her prefence brings the happy few,

Whofe deareft glory from her favour grew.

Here, in her fimple-charms, with youthful fire,　435

Proud to difplay the magic of her lyre,

Soul-foothing Harmony prefents her band :

Befide her Orpheus and Amphion ftand. .

Here, mild Philofophy, whofe thoughtful frown

Is fweetly fhaded by her olive crown,　　440

(In all her Attic elegance array'd,

Strong to convince, and gentle to perfuade)

To her, whofe breath infpir'd his every rule,

Leads the bleft fire of the Socratic fchool.

Each animating bard and moral fage,　　445

The heaven-taught minds of every clime and age,

Who foften'd manners, and refin'd the foul,

Flock to this prefence, as to glory's goal ;

And, as the mother's heart, that yearns to blefs

The rival innocents that round her prefs,　　450

Delights

Delights to fee them, as her love they fhare,
Sport in her fight, and flourifh by her care;
Fondly refponfive to their every call,
Tender of each, and provident for all:
So this fweet image of celeftial grace,   455
Who fits encircled by her lovely race,
To every fcience vital ftrength imparts,
And rears the circle of the focial arts;
With fuch folicitude fhe gives to each,
Pow'rs of fublimer aim and wider reach.   460
And now SOPHROSYNE, who near her preft,
Thus fpoke her title to her earthly gueft :—
" Behold the honour'd form, without whofe aid
My ftrength muft vanifh, and my glory fade !
Source of my being, and my life's fupport !   465
EUNOIA call'd in this celeftial court,
BENEVOLENCE the name fhe bears on earth,
The guard of weaknefs, and the friend of worth."
    She ended : and the mild maternal form
Embrac'd SERENA with a fmile as warm   470
As the gay fpirit Vegetation wears,
When fhe to crown her favourite nymph prepares,
                                        When,

When, pleas'd her flowery treasures to display,
She pours them in the lap of youthful May.

But how, SERENA! how may human speech   475
Thy heavenly raptures in this moment reach?
If aught of earthly sentiment may vie
With the pure joy these happy scenes supply,
'Tis when, unmixt with trouble and with pain,
Love glides in secret thro' the glowing vein;   480
When some fond youth, unconscious of its fire,
Free from chill fear and turbulent desire,
With every thought absorb'd in soft delight,
Sees all creation in his fair-one's sight,
And feels a blissful state without a name,   485
Repose of soul with harmony of frame.
So, plung'd in pleasure of the purest kind,
SERENA gaz'd on the maternal mind;
Gaz'd till SOPHROSYNE's directing aid
Thus summon'd to new sights th' obedient maid :—
" Haste, my fair charge, for of this ample state,   491
Tracts yet unseen thy visitation wait.
The pressing hours forbid me to unfold
Each separate province which these confines hold;

But I will lead thee to that blifsful crew, 495
Whofe kindred fpirits beft deferve thy view."
   So fpeaking, her attentive gueft fhe led
Thro' fcenes, that ftill increafing wonder bred.
Where'er fhe trod, thro' all her gorgeous feat,
Soft mufic echoed from beneath her feet : 500
Paffing a portal, on whofe lucid ftone
Emblems of innocence and beauty fhone,
They reach a lawn with verdant luftre bright,
And view the bowers of permanent delight.
No fiery fun here forms a fcorching noon, 505
No baleful meteor gleams, no chilling moon :
But, from a latent fource, one foothing light,
Whofe conftant rays repel the mift of night,
Tho' tender, chearful, and tho' warm, ferene,
Gives lafting beauty to the lovely fcene. 510
No fenfual thought this paradife profanes ;
For here tried excellence in triumph reigns,
Benignant cares eternal joy fupply,
And blifs angelic beams in every eye.
   " In yonder groups," the leading fpirit cried, 515
" My fav'rite females fee, my faireft pride.

                                        The

The firſt in rank is that diſtinguiſh'd train,
Whoſe ſtrength of ſoul was tried by Hymen's chain:
Tho' beauty bleſt their form, and love, their guide,
Their nuptial band with happieſt omens tied,   520
Beauty and love, they felt, may loſe the art
To fix inconſtant man's eccentric heart;
Yet, conſcious of their lord's neglected vow,
No virtue frown'd outrageous on their brow,
To keep returning tenderneſs aloof,   525
By coarſe upbraiding, and deſpis'd reproof:
With ſorrow ſmother'd in attraction's ſmile,
They ſtrove the ſenſe of miſery to beguile;
And, from wild paſſion's perilous abyſs,
Lure the loſt wanderer back to faithful bliſs.   530
See mild Octavia o'er this band preſide,
Voluptuous Antony's neglected bride,
Whoſe feeling heart, with all a mother's care,
Rear'd the young offspring of a rival fair.
Far other trials rais'd yon lovely crew,   535
Tho' in connubial ſcenes their merit grew:
It was their chance, ere judgment was mature,
When glittering toys the infant mind allure,

Following

Following their parents' avaricious rule,
To wed, with hopes of blifs, a wealthy fool.   540
When time remov'd delufion's veil by ftealth,
And fhow'd the drear vacuity of wealth;
When fad experience prov'd the bitter fate
Of beauty coupled to a fenfelefs mate,
Thefe gentle wives ftill gloried to fubmit;   545
Thefe, tho' invited by alluring wit,
Refus'd in paths of lawlefs joy to range,
Nor murmur'd at the lot they could not change:
But, with a lively fweetnefs, unoppreft
By a dull hufband's lamentable jeft,   550
Their conftant rays of gay good-humour fpread
A guardian glory round their idiot's head.
The next in order are thofe lovely forms,
Whofe patience weather'd all paternal ftorms;
By filial cares, the mind's unfailing teft,   555
Well have they earn'd thefe feats of blifsful reft:
They, unrepining at fevere reftraint,
Peevifh commands, and undeferv'd complaint;
Bent with unwearied kindnefs to appeafe
Each fancied want of querulous difeafe;   560
                                        Gave

Gave up thofe joys which youthful hearts engage,
To watch the weaknefs of parental age.

    Turn to this chearful band; and mark in this,
Spirits who juftly claim my realms of blifs!
Moft lovely thefe! when judg'd by generous truth, 565
Tho' beauty is not their's, nor blooming youth:
For thefe are they, who, in life's thorny fhade,
Repin'd not at the name of ancient maid.
No proud difdain, no narrownefs of heart,
Held them from Hymen's tempting rites apart; 570
But fair difcretion led them to withdraw
From the priz'd honour of his proffer'd law;
To quit the object of no hafty choice,
In mild fubmiffion to a parent's voice;
The valued lover with a figh refign,   575
And facrifice delight at duty's fhrine.
With fmiles they bore, from angry fpleen exempt,
Injurious mockery, and coarfe contempt:
'Twas their's to clafp, each felfifh care above,
A fifter's orphans with parental love,   580
And all her tender offices fupply,
Tho' bound not by the ftrong maternal tie:

                        'Twas

'Twas their's to bid inteftine quarrels ceafe,
And form the cement of domeftic peace.
No throbbing joy their fpotlefs bofom fir'd, 585
Save what benevolence herfelf infpir'd ;
No praife they fought, except that praife refin'd,
Which the heart whifpers to the worthy mind.

　　Such are thefe gentle tribes, the happy few
Who fhare the triumph to their victory due : 590
Angelic aims their fpotlefs minds employ,
And fill their meafure of unchequer'd joy.
Behold ! where fome with generous ardour wait
Around yon feer, who holds the book of fate ;
Thofe awful leaves with eager glance they turn, 595
Thence with celeftial zeal they fondly learn
What dangers threaten, thro' the vale of earth,
Their kindred pilgrims, ere they rife to birth :
To earth they ftill invifibly defcend,
In that dark fcene congenial minds defend, 600
From pleafure's bud drive fpleen's corroding worm,
And in my votaries' heart my power confirm.

　　Delights more calm yon liftening band employ,
Who deeply drink of intellectual joy.

7

See

See them around that fpeaking nymph rejoice,   605
Their pleafures varying with her varied voice !
What graces in the fweet enthufiaft glow !
Repeating here whate'er fhe learns below.
Memory her name, her charge o'er earth to flit,
And cull the faireft flowers of human wit.   610
Whatever Genius, in his happieft hour,
Has penn'd, of moral grace and comic power,
To warm the heart, the fpells of Spleen unbind,
And pour gay funfhine o'er the mifty mind;
Teach men to cherifh their fraternal tie,   615
And view kind nature with a filial eye ;
This active fpirit catches in her flight,
Skill'd to retain, and happy to recite.
Here fhe delivers each bright work, and each
Derives new beauty from her graceful fpeech.   620
Warpt by no envy, by no love mifled,
Equal fhe holds the living and the dead ;
Alike rehearfing, as they claim their turn,
The fong of Anftey, and the tale of Sterne.
     But morning calls thee hence.—Yet one fcene
          more,   625
My foftering love fhall lead thee to explore.
                                        This,

This, thy laſt ſight, with careful eyes ſurvey,
And mark th' extenſive nature of my ſway."
   Thus with fond zeal the guardian Spirit ſaid,
And to new precinĉts of her palace led ;   630
The ſcene ſhe enter'd of her richeſt ſtate,
Where on her voice the ſubjeĉt paſſions wait :
Here roſe a throne of living gems, ſo bright
No breath could fully their benignant light ;
This, her immortal ſeat, the gracious guide   635
Aſſum'd : her ward ſtood wondering at her ſide.
Swift as they felt their ruling Power inthron'd,
Ætherial beings, who her empire own'd,
Crowded in glittering pomp the gorgeous ſcene,
To pay their homage to their heavenly queen. 640
   Firſt came chaſte Love, whoſe ſweet harmonious
     form
Ne'er felt ſuſpicion's ſoul-convulſing ſtorm ;
No baleful arrow in his quiver lies,
No blinding veil inwraps his ſparkling eyes ;
There all the rays of varied joy unite,   645
And jointly ſhed unſpeakable delight:
With him was Friendſhip, like a virgin dreſt,
The ſoft aſbeſtos form'd her ſimple veſt,

VOL. V.   K   Whoſe

Whofe wond'rous folds, in fierceft flames entire,
Mock the vain ravage of confuming fire :　　650
Around this robe, a myftic chain fhe wore,
Each golden link a ftar of diamonds bore ;
Force could not tear the finifh'd work apart,
Nor int'reft loofe it by his fubtleft art :
But, ftrange to tell, if the prefiding Power,　　655
Who to her favourite gave this precious dower,
If kind SOPHROSYNE could fail to breathe
Her vital virtue on this magic wreath,
The parts muft fever, faithlefs to their truft,
The gold grow drofs, and every diamond duft.　660
Thefe Valour follow'd, deck'd with verdant palm,
Gracefully bold, majeftically calm.
A mingled troop fucceed, with feftive found,
Wifdom with olive, Wit with feathers crown'd ;
Here, hand in hand they move, no longer foes,　665
Their charms increafing as their union grows ;
Pure fpirits all, who hating mental ftrife,
Exalt creation, and embellifh life ;
All here attend, and, in their fovereign's praife,
Their circling forms the fong of glory raife.　　670

　　　　　　　　　　　　　　The

The bleſt SERENA drinks, with raviſh'd ear,
The melting muſic of the tuneful ſphere.
Now in its cloſe the ſoothing echoes roll
O'er her rapt fancy, and intrance her ſoul ;
Her ſenſes ſink in ſoft oblivion's bands,   675
Till faithful Jenny at her pillow ſtands,
Recalls each mental and corporeal power,
While ſhe proclaims aloud the paſſing hour ;
And, in a voice expreſſive of ſurpriſe,
Too ſhrill to ſeem the muſic of the ſkies,   680
Informs the ſtartled fair 'tis time to riſe.

END OF THE FIFTH CANTO.

CANTO VI.

BLEST be the heart of fympathetic mould,
    Whatever form that gentle heart infold,
Whofe generous fibres with fond terror fhake,
When keen affliction threatens to o'ertake
Young artlefs beauty, as alarm'd fhe ftrays   5
Thro' the ftrange windings of this mortal maze !
To fuch, SERENA, be thy ftory known,
Whofe bofom beft can make thy lot their own,
And, kindly fharing in thy trials paft,
Attend with fweet anxiety the laft.   10
The hour approaches, the tremendous hour,
In whofe dark moments deeper perils lower ;
Still fo inwrapt in pleafure's gay difguife,
They lurk invifible to caution's eyes ;
And, unfufpected by the fair one, wait   15
To cancel or confirm her blifsful fate.
    Her lively mind with bright ideas ftor'd,
She takes her ftation at the breakfaft-board ;

                                                Still

Still her foft foul the heavenly vifion fills,
And fweeter graces in her fmile inftils;   20
New hopes of triumph glide thro' every nerve,
And arm her glowing heart with firm referve;
Confcious the final trying chance impends,
To bear its force her every power fhe bends;
In her quick thought ambitious to prefage   25
How Spleen's dark agents may exert their rage,
She ponders on what perils may befall,
And fondly deems her mind a match for all.
Ah, lovely nymph! this dangerous pride forego;
Pride may betray—fecurity's thy foe.   30
    While fancied prudence thus, a foreign gueft,
Sits doubly cherifh'd in SERENA's breaft,
Behold a billet her attention fteal,
No common arms compofe its ample feal;
Th' unfolding paper breathes a rofeate fcent,   35
Sweet harbinger of joy, its kind intent.
Of courteous FILLIGREE it bears the name,
Clear fymptom of the peer's increafing flame!
The gracious earl, lamenting pleafure loft,
And fair SERENA in her wifhes croft,   40

K 3   Has

Has plann'd, in honour of the lovely maid,
A fancied ball, a private mafquerade,
And fupplicates her fire, with warm efteem,
To fmile indulgent on the feftive fcheme.
All arts he ufes to infure the grant,   45
Nor leaves unafk'd the eager maiden aunt.
Quick at the found SERENA's glowing heart
Throbs with gay hopes; but foon thofe hopes depart:
Reflection, in her foul a faithful guard,
The opening avenues of pleafure barr'd: 50
She deem'd the plan of this delightful fhow,
But the new ambufh of her fecret foe;
The blifs too bright to realize, fhe guefs'd,
And chas'd th' idea from her guarded breaft.
While thefe difcreet refolves her thought employ,   55
Tranquil fhe triumphs o'er her fmother'd joy.
Not fo the knight—to his parental eyes,
In dazzling pomp delufive vifions rife:
That coronet, the object of his vow,
He fees fufpended o'er his daughter's brow;   60
Eager he burns to fnap the pendent thread,
And fix the glory on his darling's head.

Far

Far wifer aims the ancient maiden caught,
No empty gew-gaw flutters in her thought ;
But, while more keenly fhe applauds the plan,   65
Her hope is folid and fubftantial man ;
Not for her infant niece, whofe baby frame
She holds unfit for Hymen's holy flame ;
But for her riper felf, whofe ftrength 'may bear
The heavieft burden of connubial care.   70

   Tho' different phantoms dance before their fight,
Niece, aunt, and father, in one wifh unite,
To join the banquet is their common choice,
The bufinefs paft with no diffenting voice ;
And the warm fire, in whom ambition burn'd,   75
A note of grateful courtefy return'd :
His billet feal'd, the glad good-humour'd knight
Launch'd forth, like Neftor, on his youthful
    might :—
" O could I now, in fpite of age, retain
That active vigour, and that fprightly vein,   80
Which led me once the lively laugh to raife
Among the merrier wits of former days,

When

When rival beauties would around me throng,
And gay ridottos liften to my fong !
Such were I now, as on the feftive night,   85
When Ch——h's charms amaz'd the public fight;
When the kind fair one, in a veil fo thin
That the clear gauze was but a lighter fkin,
Mafk'd like a virgin juft prepar'd to die,
Gave her plump beauties to each greedy eye !   90
On that fam'd night (for then with frolic fire
Youth fill'd my heart, and humour ftrung my lyre),
Pleas'd in the funfhine of her fmile to bafk,
I danc'd around her in a devil's mafk ;
And idly chanted an infernal ode,   95
In praife of all this female tempter fhow'd.
The jocund crowd, who throng'd with me to gaze,
Extoll'd my unpremeditated lays,
And Sport, who ftill of this old revel brags,
*Styl'd her the firft of maids, and me of wags; 100
Then a light devil, now, reduc'd to limp,
I am but fit to play the hag-born imp ;

* Θεων Διι, Νεςορι τ' ανδρων.
                    See Neftor's fpeech in the 11th Iliad.

                                        Still,

Still, not to crofs the frolic of this ball,
Still as the tortoife Caliban I'll crawl,
And if with gout my burning ankles flinch,　　105
. I'll call it Profpero's tormenting pinch;
Still in this fhape I'll fhow them what I am :
And PEN. fhall go as Sycorax my dam."

So fpoke the knight; and fpoke with fo much weight,
The liftening females faw his word was fate;　　110
For ne'er did Jove with fo refolv'd a brow
To fmiling Love his joyous fcheme avow,
When he concerted, for his fpecial mirth,
A mafquerading on the ftage of earth,
And of the fwan's foft plume, or bull's rough hair,
Order'd the fancy-drefs he chofe to wear.　　116 .
From whence let fapient antiquarians fhow
The ancient ufe of mafquerades below.
SERENA fmil'd to fee this joyous fire
Infufe new youth in her determin'd fire;　　120
But mute PENELOPE, with half a figh,
" With one aufpicious and one dropping eye,"
Heard the firm knight his fixt refolve impart,
Tickling at once and torturing her heart.

　　　　　　　　　　　　　The

The ball fhe relifh'd, but abhorr'd the tafk   125
To hide her beauties in a beldam's mafk:
Miranda's name would better fuit her plan,
A fimple maiden, not afraid of man ;
But us'd, alas ! her brother's law to feel,
She knows that law admits not of repeal.   130
Trufting her charms will any garb enrich,
She deigns to take the habit of a witch.
Never did forcerefs in the fhades of night
Try to illuminate a filthy fprite
With fonder efforts, or with worfe fuccefs,   135
Than PEN. now labour'd, in this wayward drefs,
To give the fprightly fhow of living truth
To the poor ghoft of her departed youth.
As witches o'er their magic cauldron bend,
Anxious to fee their menial imps afcend ;   140
So in her glafs the ancient maiden pries,
And dreams new graces in her perfon rife.
No fuch delights, whofe dear delufions pleafe,
The mild SERENA in her mirror fees ;
She, at whofe toilet beauty's latent queen   145
Attends, enchanted with her filial mien,

And

And o'er her favourite's unconſcious face
Breathes her own roſeate glow and vivid grace.
She haſtes her glittering garments to adjuſt,
With all the modeſt charms of ſweet diſtruſt,   150
Doubting that beauty, which ſhe doubts alone,
Which dazzles every eye except her own.
The native diffidence which ſway'd her mind,
Now feels new terrors with its own combin'd;
The robes of Ariel to the nymph recall   155
Thoſe diſappointments that may yet. befall;
As her fair hands the gauze or tiſſue touch,
They fondly warn her not to hope too much.
She feels the friendly counſel they impart,
And caution reigns protector of her heart.   160

   The fateful evening comes—the coach attends,
And firſt the gouty Caliban aſcends;
Then, in deformity's well-ſuited pride,
Sour Sycorax is ſtation'd by his ſide;
And laſt, with ſportive ſmiles, divinely ſweet,   165
Light Ariel perches on the vacant ſeat.
Fancy now paints the ſcene of pleaſure near,
Yet fluttering gaiety is check'd by fear.

                           Her

Her wish to view the festive sight runs high;
But the fond nymph remembers, with a sigh,   170
From hope's keen hand the cup of joy may slip,
And fall untasted, though it reach the lip.
As the fine artist, whose nice toils aspire
To fame eternal by encaustic fire;
If he, with grief, has seen the faithless heat   175
Mar the rich labour it should make compleat,
When next his hands, with trembling care, confide
To the fierce element his pencil's pride,
Watches unceasing the pernicious flame,
Terror and hope contending in his frame,   180
While his fair work the dangerous fire sustains,
Feels it in all his sympathetic veins, .
And at each trivial found that chance may cause,
Hears the gem crack, and sees its cruel flaws;
With such solicitude the panting-maid   185
Past the long street, of every noise afraid.
Now, while around her rival flambeaus flare,
And the coach rattles thro' the crowded square,
She fears some dire mischance must yet befall,
Some demon snatch her from the promis'd ball; 190.
                          And

And dreams no trial more fevere than this,
So bright fhe figures the new fcene of blifs :
Yet, horrid as it feems, her heart is bent
To bear e'en this, and bear it with content.

But, whirl'd at length within the porter's gate, 195
She thinks what perils at the ball may wait ;
And, as fhe now alights, the fluttering fair
Invokes her guardian to protect her there,
Till thoughts of danger, thoughts of caution, fly
Before the magic blaze that meets her eye. 200
Th' advancing nymph, at every ftep fhe takes,
Pants with amazement, doubtful if fhe wakes ;
Far as her eyes the glittering fcene command,
'Tis all enchantment, all a fairy land ;
No veftiges of modern pomp appear, 205
No modern melody falutes her ear :
With Moorifh notes the echoing manfion rings,
And its tranfmuted form to fancy brings
The rich * Alhambra of the Moorifh kings.
The peer, who keenly thirfts for fafhion's praife, 210
To gild his revel with no common rays,

* See the views of this palace in Swinburn's Travels.

Summon'd

Summon'd his modifh architect, whofe fkill
Can all the wifhes of caprice fulfil.
His genius, equal to the wildeft tafk,
Gave to the houfe itfelf a Gothic mafk.   215
The chaplain, that no gueft might feel neglect,
As a magician of the Arab fect,
Wav'd a prefiding wand throughout the ball,
And well provided for the wants of all.

The peer himfelf, his prowefs to evince,   220
Shines in the femblance of a Moorifh prince;
And round the brilliant mimic hero wait
All pomp and circumftance of Moorifh ftate:
Thro' all his fplendid dome no eye could find
Aught unembellifh'd, fave the mafter's mind.   225
There, tho' repreft by courtefy's controul,
Lurks the low mover of the little foul,
Mean vanity; whofe flave can never prove
The heart-refining flame of genuine love.
While her cold joys his abject mind amufe,   230
His thoughts are bufied on connubial views.
His houfe compleat, its decorations plac'd
By the fure hand of fafhionable tafte,

He

He only wants, to crown his modifh life,
That laft and fineft moveable—a wife. 235
She too muft prove, to fix his coy defire,
Such as the eye of fafhion will admire.
His ball is but a jury, to decide
Upon the merit of his fancied bride.
If fweet SERENA, on this fignal night, 240
Shines the firft idol of the public fight;
If gallantry's fixt eyes pronounce her fair,
By the fure fign of one unceafing ftare;
And if, prophetic of her nobler doom,
Each rival beauty fhudders at her bloom; 245
The die is caft—he weds—the point is clear;
She cannot flight the vows of fuch a peer.
Thus argued in his mind the feftive earl,
And, left he lightly chufe an awkward girl,
Wifely conven'd, on this important cafe, 250
Each fafhionable judge of female grace.
Here beaux efprits in various figures lurk,
Of Jew and Gentile, Bramin, Tartar, Turk;
But of the manly mafks, a youthful bard
Seem'd moft to challenge beauty's foft regard: 255

Adorn'd

Adorn'd with native elegance, he wore,

In fimpleft form, the minftrel drefs of yore:

They call him EDWIN, who around him throng,

EDWIN, immortaliz'd in Beattie's fong;

And, footh to fay, within a comely frame,   260

He bore a heart that anfwer'd to the name;

For this neat habit deck'd a generous youth,

Of gentleft manners, and fincereft truth.

'Tho' on his birth propitious fortune fmil'd,

No proud parental folly fpoil'd the child;   265

And genius, more beneficently kind,

Bleft with fuperior wealth his manly mind.

Of years he barely counted twenty-one;

But, like a brilliant morn, his opening life begun.

Fain would the mufe on this her votary dwell,   270

And fully paint the youth fhe loves fo well;

His figure's charms, the mufic of his tongue,

What nymphs his lays allur'd, what lays he fung:

But higher cares her rambling fong controul;

SERENA's perils fummon all her foul;   275

For Spleen, ambitious to exert her force,

Confcious this trial is her laft refource,

Moft

Moſt keenly bent on her pernicious taſk,
Has ſhifted round the ball from maſk to maſk,
Watching the moment, with infernal care, 280
To form with deepeſt art her final ſnare,
And manacle the mind of the unguarded fair.

It comes, the moment that muſt fix her lot,
By her, ah thoughtleſs maid ! by her forgot ;
Tho' the light Hours, e'en in their frolic ring, 285
Trembling perceive the fearful chance they bring,
And, ſhuddering at the nymph's terrific ſtate,
Seem anxious to ſuſpend her doubtful fate.

Now ſocial eaſe the place of ſport ſupplied,
The hot oppreſſive maſk was thrown aſide, 290
And beauty ſhone reveal'd in all her bluſhing pride.
Superior ſtill in features as in form,
With admiration fluſh'd, with pleaſure warm,
The gay SERENA every eye allur'd ;
The hearts her figure won her face ſecur'd : 295
A tender ſweetneſs ſtill the nymph maintain'd,
And modeſty o'er all her graces reign'd.
Well might her ſoul to brilliant hopes incline,
A thouſand youths had call'd her charms divine ;

A thouſand

A thoufand friends had whifper'd in her ear,   300
That fate had mark'd her for the feftive peer.
Her youthful fancy, tho' by pomp amus'd,
Wifh'd not thofe offers, which her heart refus'd :
That tender heart, by no vain pride poffeft,
With indecifive trembling fhook her breaft,   305
Like a young bird, that, fluttering in the air,
Wifhes to build her neft, yet knows not where.

    The bufy earl, his puny love to raife,
Hunted the circling whifper of her praife ;
Heard envy own her lovely charms, tho' loth,   310
Heard tafte atteft them with a modifh oath ;
And, nuptial projects thickening in his mind,
Now his fair partner in the dance rejoin'd.
As now the fprightly mufic paus'd, my lord
Eager refolv'd to touch a fofter chord ;   315
Secure of all repulfe, he vainly meant
Half to difplay, half hide his fond intent,
And, in diffembled paffion's flowery tropes,
To fport at leifure with the virgin's hopes :
For this he fram'd a motley fpeech, replete   320
With amorous compliment and vain conceit.

                             The

The labour'd nothing with complacent pride
He fpoke; but to his fpeech no nymph replied:
For in the moment, the loft fair devotes
Her willing ear to more attractive notes. 325
The minftrel happen'd near the nymph to walk,
Rapt with a bofom-friend in fecret talk,
And, at the inftant when the earl began
Half to unfold his matrimonial plan,
EDWIN, in whifpers, from the crowd retir'd, 330
Chanc'd to repeat the fonnet fhe infpir'd:
The founds, tho' faint, her recollection caught,
Drew her quick eye, and fixt her wondering thought.
Loft in this fweet furprife, fhe could not hear
A fingle accent of the amorous peer. 335
Spleen faw the moment that fhe fought to gain,
And perch'd triumphant on the noble's brain.
With jealous envy ftung, and baffled pride,
" Contemptuous girl!" with fudden rage, he cried,
" If here to happier youths thy views incline, 340
I want not fairer nymphs who challenge mine.
Thy breaft in vain with penitence may burn;
But, once neglected, I no more return."

L 2

Thus

Thus loudly speaking, with distemper'd heat,
Rudely he turn'd, with rancorous scorn replete. 345
SERENA, startled at th' injurious sound,
Survey'd th' insulting peer, who sternly frown'd;
Shame and resentment thro' her bosom rush,
Swell every vein, and raise the burning blush.
Love, new-born love, but in its birth conceal'd, 350
Nor to the nymph herself as yet reveal'd,
And just disdain, and anger's honest flame,
With complicated power convulse her frame:
Contending passions every thought confound,
And in tumultuous doubt her soul is drown'd. 355
Now treacherous pride, who tempts her tongue to trip,
Forms to a keen reply her quivering lip:
Insidious Spleen now hovers o'er the fair,
Deems her half lock'd within her hateful snare;
In her new slave preparing to rejoice, 360
To taint her spirit, and untune her voice.
Hapless SERENA! what can save thee now?
The fiend's dark signet stamps thy clouded brow,
In thy swoln eye I see the starting drop;
This fatal shower, ætherial guardian! stop: 365

Haste

Hafte to thy votary, hafte, her foul fuftain,
Nor let the trials fhe has paft be vain.
Ah me ! while yet I fpeak, with fhuddering dread
I hear the magic girdle's burfting thread.
This horrid omen, ye kind powers! avert :   370
Nor thou, bright zone ! thy brighter charge defert.
Ah, fruitlefs prayer ! her panting breaft behold !
See ! the gauze fhakes in many a ruffled fold !
Forc'd from their ftation by her heaving heart,
From the ftrain'd girdle thrice three fpangles ftart :
Thro' her diforder'd drefs a pafs they've found,   376
And fallen, fee, they glitter on the ground !—
O bleffed chance ! with life-recalling light
The glittering monitors attract her fight !
Like ftars emerging from the darken'd pole,   380
They fparkle fafety to her harrafs'd foul.
See ! from her brow the clouds of trouble fly,
Vexation's tear is vanifh'd from her eye !
Her rofy cheeks with joy's foft radiance burn,
Like nature fmiling at the fun's return ;   385
The nymph, no more with mental darknefs blind,
Shines the fweet ruler of her refcu'd mind.

Hence,

Hence, hateful Spleen! thy fancied prize refign,.
Renounce for ever what fhall ne'er be thine;
For, confcious of her airy guardian's aid,   390
She feels new fpirit thro' her heart convey'd,
And, inly blefling this victorious hour,
Her foul exults in its recover'd power.
In fuch mild terms fhe hails th' infulting peer,
As Spleen, if mortal, muft expire to hear;   395
But, driven for ever from the lovely girl,
The foul fiend riots in the captive earl.
He an'wers not; but, with a fullen air,
On happier EDWIN, who approach'd the fair,
Darts fuch a glance of rage and envious hate,   400
As Satan caft on Eden's blifsful ftate,
When on our parents firft he fixt his fight,
And undelighted gaz'd on all delight:
So doom'd to look, and doom'd fuch pangs to feel,
Scornful he turn'd on his elaftic heel.   405

   " O lovely mildnefs! oh angelic maid!
Deferving homage, tho' to fcorn betray'd;

    5   Rife

Rife ftill, fweet fpirit, rife thefe wrongs above,
Turn from injurious pride to faithful love ;
Tho' on my brow no coronet may fhine,   410
Wealth I can offer at thy beauty's fhrine,
And, worthier thee, a heart that worfhips thine."
Thus, with new-kindled love's afpiring flame,
Spoke the fond youth conceal'd by EDWIN's name,
The gallant FALKLAND, rich in inborn worth, 415
By fortune bleft, and not of abject birth.
Warmly he fpoke, with that indignant heat
With which the generous heart ne'er fails to beat,
When worth infulted wakens virtuous ire,
And injur'd beauty fets the foul on fire.   420
Quick to his voice the ftartled virgin turn'd,
With wonder, hope, and joy, her bofom burn'd ;
With fweet confufion, flurried and amaz'd,
On his attractive form fhe wildly gaz'd.
Full on her thought the friendly vifions rufh'd ; 425
Blufhing fhe view'd him, view'd him ftill and
          blufh'd ;
And, foft affection quickening at the fight,
Perchance had fwoon'd with fullnefs of delight,

But that her father's voice, with quick controul,
Recall'd the functions of her fainting foul.   430
When on the diftant feat, where, fondly fixt,
He view'd the nymph as in the dance fhe mixt,
He indiftinctly heard, with wounded ear,
The fpleenful outrage of the angry peer,
Swift at th' imperfect found, with choler wild,   435
He fprung to fuccour his infulted child ;
But ere his fury into language broke,
Love calm'd the ftorm that arrogance awoke.
The fudden burft of FALKLAND's tender flame,
His winning manners, his diftinguifh'd name,   440
His liberal foul, by fortune's fmile careft,
All join'd to harmonize the father's breaft.
His fiery thoughts fubfide in glad furprife,
And to the generous youth he warmly cries :
" Ingenuous FALKLAND ! by thy franknefs won, 445
My willing heart would own thee as my fon ;
But on thy hopes SERENA muft decide :—
Hafte we together from this houfe of pride."
   So fpoke the fire ; for, to her votary kind,
SOPHROSYNE infpir'd his foften'd mind.   450

Speaking;

Speaking, he fmil'd, to fee that on his word
The lover hung, and bleft the founds he heard ;
That his embarrafs'd child his fentence caught
With each tumultuous fign of tender thought ;
Whofe blufhes, fpringing from the heart, declare 455
The dawn of fondnefs in the modeft fair.
Th' enchanted youth with ecftafy convey'd
Forth from the troubled feaft the trembling maid.

   As the keen failor, whom his daring foul
Has drawn, too vent'rous, near the freezing pole ; 460
Who, having flighted caution's tame advice,
Seems wedg'd within impervious worlds of ice ;
If, from each chilling form of peril free,
At length he reach the unincumber'd fea,
With joy fuperior to his tranfient pain,   465
Rufhes, exulting, o'er th' expanfive main :
Such ftrong delight SERENA's bofom fhar'd,
When fweet reflection to her heart declar'd,
That all the trials of her fate were paft,
And love's decifive plaudit feal'd the laft.   470
Her airy guard prepares the fofteft down,
From peace's wing, to line the nuptial crown :

Her

Her smiles accelerate the bridal morn,
And clear her votary's path from every thorn.
On the quick match the prude's keen censures fall, 475
Blind to the heavenly power who guided all:
But mild SERENA scorn'd the prudish play,
To wound warm love with frivolous delay;
Nature's chaste child, not affectation's slave,
The heart she meant to give, she frankly gave. 480
Thro' her glad sire no gouty humours run,
Jocund he glories in his destin'd son.
PENELOPE herself, no longer seen
In the sour semblance of tormenting Spleen,
Buys for her niece the robes of nuptial state,   485
Nor scolds the mercer once thro' all the long debate.
For quick dispatch, the honest man of law
Toils half the night the legal ties to draw;
At length th' enraptur'd youth, all forms compleat,
Bears his sweet bride to his paternal seat;   490
On a fair lawn the chearful mansion stood,
And high behind it rose a circling wood.
As the blest lord of this extensive reign
Led his dear partner thro' her new domain,

With

With fond furprife, SERENA foon defcried   495

A temple rais'd to her ætherial guide.

Its ornaments fhe view'd with tender awe,

Their fafhion fuch as fhe in vifion faw ;

For the kind youth, her grateful fmile to gain,

Had, from her clear defcription, deck'd the fane. 500

Joyful he cried, to his angelic wife,

" Be this kind power the worfhip of our life !"

He fpoke ; and led her to the inmoft fhrine ;

Here, link'd in rofy bands, two votaries fhine ;

The pencil had imparted life to each,   505

With energy that feem'd beyond its reach.

Firft ftood Connubial Love, a manly youth,

Whofe bright eye fpoke the ardent vows of truth ;

Friendfhip, fweet fmiling, fill'd the fecond place,

In all the fofter charms of virgin grace.   510

Their meeting arms a myftic tablet raife,

Deck'd with thefe lines, the moral of my lays :—

" VIRTUE's an ingot of Peruvian gold,

SENSE the bright ore Potofi's mines unfold ;

But TEMPER's image muft their ufe create,   515

And give thefe precious metals fterling weight."

P L A Y S

OF

T H R E E   A C T S;

WRITTEN FOR A

PRIVATE THEATRE.

T O

HER GRACE THE DUTCHESS OF
DEVONSHIRE.

Non perch' io creda bifognar miei carmi
A chi fe ne fa copia da fe fteffa ;
Ma fol per fatisfare a quefto mio
Che ho d' onorarla e di ledar difio.

ARIOSTO, Canto xxxvii.

THE Great and Fair, in every age and clime,

Receive free homage from the Sons of Rhyme :

Bend, ye ambitious Bards, at Grandeur's fhrine!

Be Power your patron ! Wit and Beauty mine !—

To thee, whom elegance has taught to pleafe

By ferious dignity, or fportive eafe ;

Whom

Whom Virtue hails, at Pleafure's feftive rites,

Chafté Arbiter of Art's refin'd delights :

To thee, fair DEVON! I breathe this votive

    ftrain ;

Nor dread th' averted ear of proud Difdain :

For O, if mufic has not bleft my lyre,

A lovelier fpirit of th' ætherial choir,

Joy-breathing Gratitude, that hallow'd gueft,

Who fires with heavenly zeal the human breaft,

Bids my weak voice her fwelling note prolong,

And confecrate to thee her tributary fong.

  When firft my anxious Mufe's fav'rite child,

Her young SERENA, artlefs, fimple, wild,

                      Prefum'd

Prefum'd from privacy's fafe fcenes to fly,

And met in giddy hafte the public eye;

Thy generous praife her trembling youth fuf-

    tain'd,

The fmile fhe dar'd not afk, from thee fhe gain'd;

And found a guardian in the gracious DEVON,

Kind as the regent of her fancied heaven.——

The flatter'd Mufe, whofe offspring thou haft bleft,

In the fond pride that rules a parent's breaft,

Prefents thus boldly to thy kind embrace

This little group of her fucceeding race.

Bleft! if by pathos true to Nature's law,

From thy foft bofom they may haply draw

Thofe tender fighs, that eloquently fhow

The virtues of the heart from whence they flow!

Bleft! if by foibles humorously hit,

In the light scenes that aim at comic wit,

They turn thy pensive charms to mirthful

    grace,

And wake the sprightly sweetness of thy face!

While thus the proud Enthusiast would

    aspire

To change thy beauties with her changing lyre;

Much as she wants the talent and the right,

To shew thy various charms in varied light,

O might the Muse, intruding on thy bower,

From her fair Patron catch the magic power

Frequent to meet the public eye, and still

That fickle eye with fond amazement fill!

                      Let

Let her, if this vain wish is lost in air,

Breathe from her grateful heart a happier

    prayer !—

Howe'er her different fables may give birth

To fancied woe, and visionary mirth;

May all thy griefs belong to Fiction's reign,

And wound thee only with a pleasing pain !

May thy light spirit, on the sea of life,

Elude the rocks of care, the gusts of strife,

And safely, as the never-sinking buoy,

Float on th' unnebbig flood of real joy !

EARTHAM.
January 29th, 1784.

           W. HAYLEY.

      M 2   PREFACE.

PREFACE.

AS the following Plays were intended only for a private theatre, I have been tempted by that circumstance to introduce a kind of novelty into our language, by writing three comedies in rhyme, though the Comic Muse of our country has been long accustomed to express herself in prose, and her custom has the sanction of settled precept, and successful example. The Antiquarian, indeed, may remind me that Gammer Gurton's Needle, one of the earliest of our old plays, with other comic productions of that rude period, was written in rhyme; and possibly some fastidious enemies of that Gothic jingle, as they affect to call it, may consider the present Publication as nothing more than a relapse into the most barbarous mode of dramatic composition.

For

For the boldnefs of an attempt, which has no modern precedent to plead in its behalf, fome apology may be due to the Public.

In the firft place, I beg it may not be fuppofed, that by writing a comedy in rhyme, I mean to convey an indirect cenfure on the contrary practice. No one can prize more highly than I do the many excellent comedies in profe, with which our language is enriched. I am very far from entertaining a wifh to overturn the ceremonial which the Comic Mufe of England has eftablifhed; but I hope to find our country as much a friend to toleration in the forms of literature, as in thofe of religion. The cuftom of other enlightened nations, both ancient and modern, may be pleaded on this occafion in behalf of verfe. Ariftophanes, in his play of the Clouds, feems to pride himfelf on his poetry. Ariofto having written two comedies in profe, converted them both into metre at a maturer period of his life; and Moliere, the unrivalled mafter of the French comic theatre, who has written admirably both in profe and rhyme, is, I think, moft admirable, and moft truly comic, when he adheres to the latter.

To

To the author who attempts a comedy in English rhyme, our language seems to offer an advantage, which the French poet did not enjoy. The Comic Muse of France has chiefly confined herself to that structure of verse, which belongs equally to her Tragic Sister. In the poetry of our nation, this particular measure is appropriated to sportive subjects, and though hitherto not used in Comedy, it possesses to an English ear a very comic vivacity. That it is highly calculated for poems of wit and humour, we have a striking proof in that most exquisite production the Bath Guide. How far it may succeed through the varied scenes of an English play, experiment only can determine. As some readers, on the first sight of a comedy in rhyme, may hastily suppose that the fashion and the materials of the work are borrowed from the Theatre of France, I think it proper to declare, in justice to the writers of that country, that they are by no means answerable for any defects which may be found in these dramatic performances. I am not conscious of having borrowed a single character or situation from any comic writer whatever, either foreign or domestic.——The first of the

M 4 three

three comedies, contained in the present Publication, was founded on a real anecdote related to me by an intimate friend, who, concealing the names of the parties, mentioned their ludicrous adventure as a new and tempting subject for the Comic Muse.——The plan of the second arose in the mind of its author, from his remarking the various effects of Connoisseurship in different characters. An attachment to the fine arts, which is allowed to refine and strengthen the virtues of a manly and a generous spirit, has perhaps a peculiar tendency not only to shew, but to increase the narrowness of a vain and feeble mind; and if such a tendency exists, it is the province of a comic writer to counteract and correct it.——The aim of the third comedy in this collection is to laugh at two distinct species of affectation, very prevalent in our age and country; the affectation of refined sentiment, and the affectation of pompous and pedantic expression. I protest however against personal application: and, to guard against it, let me declare, that this ridicule is levelled, not at the great and respectable Veteran in the field of literature, whose phrases may sometimes be borrowed by a character in

the

the play ; but at the namelefs and fervile herd of his awkward imitators.—Vigor and originality of thought give a fanction to the pomp and peculiarity of his language. If fingularities of ftyle are united with genius and moral excellence, they are properly regarded with a partial refpect ; but when thefe fingularities are prepofteroufly copied, and feem to prevail as a fafhion, they become, I apprehend, very fair fubjects of fportive fatire.

When I reflect what long and eftablifhed prejudice a rhyming play muft encounter—when I remember that even Dryden himfelf, the moft able advocate, and the greateft mafter of rhyme in our language, has exprefsly condemned the ufe of it in comedy—I am alarmed at the hardinefs of my attempt ; but when I recollect that time, the moft infallible teft of literary opinion, has fully fhewn the miftake of that immortal Poet, in recommending the ufe of rhyme in Englifh Tragedy, I am inclined to hope that he might be equally miftaken in fuppofing it utterly unfuited to our Comic Mufe. It may be urged indeed, with great truth, that a comedy in rhyme cannot be fo clofe a copy of Nature as a comedy

medy in profe, the latter adhering to the very language of common life. But from a fifter-art we may borrow, at leaft a plaufible argument in favour of Poetry, on the prefent occafion. The great mafter, who has defcanted fo happily on the principles of Painting, obferves with great propriety, in one of his difcourfes, that " we are " not always pleafed with the moft abfolute poffible re- " femblance of an imitation to its original object : cafes " may exift, in which fuch a refemblance may be even " difagreeable. I fhall only obferve, that the effect of " figures in wax-work, though certainly a more exact " reprefentation than can be given by painting or fculp- " ture, is a fufficient proof that the pleafure we receive " from imitation is not increafed merely in proportion " as it approaches to minute and detailed reality : we " are pleafed, on the contrary, by feeing ends anfwered " by feeming inadequate means *."—On thefe prin- ciples, which perhaps are equally juft in the two kindred arts, a comedy in Rhyme may be ftill more entertaining than a comedy, of equal merit in other points, which confines itfelf to profe ; and a critic who exclaims againft

* Sir Jofhua Reynolds' Difcourfe of December 1782.

6

the

the unnatural effect of a rhyming dialogue, may as justly censure a portrait on canvass, because it is not so exact a copy of life, as an image of coloured wax. In both cases, the artist, whether painter or poet, may be justly called a true and a pleasing copier of Nature, if he preserves as high a degree of resemblance, as his mode of imitation will admit, and embellishes his work with the attractive and almost indispensable graces of ease, spirit, and freedom.

It is said by Voltaire of theatrical composition in general, " Tous les genres sont bons hors le genre en- " nuyeux." If the present comedies fall not within the class which that lively Writer has so justly proscribed, the Author may be allowed to hope, that his liberal and enlightened readers will look with indulgence on a Pub- lication, which arose from his wish to introduce a strik- ing, and he trusts not a blamable, variety into the amusements of English literature.

THE

THE

HAPPY PRESCRIPTION;

OR, THE

LADY RELIEVED FROM HER LOVERS:

A COMEDY, IN RHYME.

Persons of the Drama.

SIR NICHOLAS ODDFISH,
SAPPHIC,
DECISIVE,
MORLEY,
COLONEL FELIX,
JONATHAN, Servant to MORLEY;

SELINA, Niece to SIR NICHOLAS,
MRS. FELIX, her Cousin, and Wife to the
      COLONEL,
JENNY, Servant to SELINA.

Servants *of* SIR NICHOLAS, *&c.*

SCENE *the Country Mansion of the* ODDFISH *Family.*

THE
HAPPY PRESCRIPTION.

ACT I.

SCENE I.

Enter Sir Nicholas, *in debate with* Mrs. Felix
and Selina.

MRS. FELIX.

WHAT a ſtrange declaration !— it gives me the
ſpleen ;
But 'tis what good Sir Nicholas never can mean.

SIR NICHOLAS.

Not mean it, fair Lady !—by Jupiter, yes !
And my projeᴄt, you'll ſee, will be crown'd with ſucceſs ;
I am joyous myſelf, and 'tis ever my plan
To give thoſe I love all the joy that I can.

MRS.

MRS. FELIX.

We own it—but joy is like diet, dear Coufin,
One palate mayn't relifh what pleafes a dozen;
Nor will I allow that my appetite's vicious,
If perchance I don't like, what you think moft delicious.

SIR NICHOLAS.

Rare dainty diftinctions !—But can I believe
That a woman e'er liv'd, fince the wedding of Eve,
Whofe heart (tho' moft coyly her head might be car-
        ried)
Did not fervently wifh to be fpeedily married ?
Not to wound your nice ears with the name of defires
Which youth renders lovely, and nature infpires,
Your fex, from its weaknefs, demands a defender,
Whom pride and affection make watchful and tender;
And if my fair Coz is no hypocrite grown,
The truth of my maxims you'll honeftly own;
While the wars from your arms the brave Colonel detain,
Is the want of a hufband the fource of no pain ?

MRS. FELIX.

There, indeed, you have touch'd me a little too near,
My Soldier, you know, to my foul is moft dear;
I own—and my franknefs you never will blame,
I'd purchafe his prefence with aught but his fame.

SIR

SIR NICHOLAS.

Well faid, thou dear, honeft, and warm-hearted wife;
For thy truth may good angels ftill watch o'er his life,
And while others the rough field of flaughter are tread-
      ing,
Send him home full of glory, to dance at our wedding!
For a wedding we'll have to enliven us all,
And Hymen's bright altar fhall warm the old hall.
For my Niece ere I die 'tis my wifh to provide,
And ere two months are paft I *will* fee her a bride.
I'm refolv'd—and you know that my neighbours all fay,
Sir Nicholas Oddfifh will have his own way.

MRS. FELIX.

Selina, dear Sir, wants no other protection,
While her life glides in peace by your gentle direction.
She thinks, and, I own, I approve her remark,
In conjugal cares 'tis too foon to embark:
Her bofom untouch'd by Love's dangerous dart,
Fate has not yet fhewn her the man of her heart.

SIR NICHOLAS.

The man of her heart!—thefe nonfenfical fancies
You light-headed females pick out of romances.
That I am no tyrant you know very well,
So, Coufin, don't teach my good Niece to rebel!

I am no greedy guardian, who thinks it his duty

On the altar of Plutus to facrifice beauty ;

Whofe venal barbarity, juftly abhorr'd,

Ties a lovely young girl to an old crippled lord,

And bafely, to gain either rank or eftate,

Make her fwear fhe will love, what fhe cannot but hate.

From fuch a protector Heaven guard my dear Niece !

I wifh her to wed that her joys may increafe ;

And the deuce muft be in the ftrange girl who difco-

　　　vers

No man to her mind in fuch plenty of lovers.

To no very great length will my cruelty run,

If from twenty admirers I bid her chufe one.

　　　　　　M R S. F E L I X.

But why, dear Sir Nicholas, why in fuch hafte ?

　　　　　S I R N I C H O L A S.

'Tis thus that my projects are ever difgrac'd

With the falfe names of hurry and precipitation,

Becaufe I abhor filly procraftination ;

That thief of delight, who deludes all our fenfes,

Who cheats us for ever with idle pretences,

By whom, like the dog in the fable, betray'd,

We let go the fubftance to fnap at the fhade.

To feize prefent time is the true art of life ;
'Tis Time who now cries, make Selina a wife !
The feafon is come, I've fo long wifh'd to fee
From the moment I dandled her firft on my knee :
She, you know, to my care was bequeath'd by my
   Brother,
And having this child, I ne'er wifh'd for another :
Thro' life I have kept myfelf fingle for her ;
Her intereft, her joy, to my own I prefer.

SELINA.

Your kindnefs, dear Sir, I can never repay.

SIR NICHOLAS.

In truth, my dear damfel, you eafily may ;
I demand no return fo enormoufly great ;
I afk but a boy to poffefs my eftate.

SELINA.

Lord, Uncle, how come fuch odd thoughts in your
   head ?

MRS. FELIX.

From his heart, I affure you—'tis pleafantly faid ;
A fair ftipulation—both parties agreed,
The compact, I truft, in due time will fucceed :
But patience, dear Knight, you will have your defire,
Nor wait very long for a young little 'fquire.

N 2

SIR NICHOLAS.

The cold ftream of Patience ne'er creeps in my veins,
But the wifh my heart forms my quick fpirit attains.
I'm none of your chill atmofpherical wretches,
Whofe affections are fubject to ftarts and to catches;
Whofe wifh, like a weather-cock, veering about,
Now turns towards hope, and now changes to doubt:
No, mine, like the needle without variation,
Only looks to one point, and that point's Confumma-
          tion.
I want to behold this young urchin arife,
Before I have loft or my legs or my eyes,
That I may enjoy all his little vagaries,
As the changeable feafon of infancy varies.
I long to be moulding his heart and his fpirit;
To fhew him the fields he is born to inherit;
Lead him round our rich woods, while my limbs are
          yet limber,
And tell the young rogue how I've nurs'd up his timber;
That when the worn thread of my life is untwifted,
He long may remember that I have exifted;
And when my old frame in our monument refts,
As he walks by my grave with a few worthy guefts,

                              He

He thus to fome warm-hearted friend may addrefs him,
Here lies my odd, honeft, old Uncle—God blefs him !

MRS. FELIX.

Thank Heaven, dear Coufin, your hale conftitution
Shews not the leaft fign of a near diffolution.

SELINA.

To make your life happy, whate'er the condition,
Has been, my dear Uncle, my higheft ambition ;
To fulfil every wifh that your fancy can frame,
Still is, as it ought to be, ever my aim :
But if by your voice I am doom'd to the altar,
With terror and pain my weak accents muft falter,
Unlefs my kind ftars a new lover fhould fend me,
Unlike all the fwains who now deign to attend me.

SIR NICHOLAS.

Nice wench ! do you want the whole world to adore
   . you ?
Would you have all the men of the earth rang'd be-
   fore you ?
For, thanks to your charms, and to fortune's kind
   bounty,
You may rank in your train all the youth of our county ;
And, chufe whom you will, if the man has but worth,
And is nearly your equal in wealth and in birth,

N 3   I give

I give my confent—you are free from reftriction;
But I will not be plagu'd with perverfe contradiction,
I will fee you wed without any delay :
Your two fitteft lovers are coming to-day ;
Young Sapphic, whofe verfes delight all the fair,
And Dicky Decifive, Sir Jacob's next heir :
Both young and both wealthy, both comely and clever,
To gain you, no doubt, each will warmly endeavour ;
For they come for a month, by my own invitation,
On purpofe to found my dear girl's inclination :
I have faid to them both, and no man can fpeak fairer,
Let him, who can pleafe her moft, win her and wear her,

SELINA, *afide to* Mrs. Felix.

Good angels defend me !

MRS. FELIX.

I fee nothing frightful :
Our month with fuch guefts muft be very delightful :
When Sapphic's foft verfes incline us to dofe,
Dick will keep us awake with fatirical profe.

SIR NICHOLAS.

Don't crofs me, I fay ! nor miflead my good Niece !
By Jove, if fhe thwarts me with any caprice,
Like a certain old Juftice, I'll ring up my maids,
And marry the firft of the frank-hearted jades ;

For

For perverſe contradiction I never will bear,
But provide for myſelf a more dutiful heir.

Mrs. Felix.

Dear Couſin, in ſpite of his Worſhip's deciſion,
You cannot be certain of ſuch a proviſion :
Attempts of that nature are ſubject to fail.

Sir Nicholas.

My deſigns, you ſhall ſee, Madam, always prevail :
For if this nice Gipſy, by your machination,
Declines every offer, to give me vexation,
Like my late jolly neighbour, Sir Timothy Trickum,
Who vindictively married the frail Molly Quickum,
I'll make ſure of the matter, and chuſe me a wife,
With an heir ready plac'd on the threſhold of life :
For, as I have ſaid, tho' a foe to reſtriction,
I never will ſuffer perverſe contradiction.
You now know my mind, which no maſk ever covers,
So farewell, and prepare to receive your two lovers.

[*Exit.*

Mrs. Felix.

Go thy way, thou ſtrange mixture of ſenſe and of
        blindneſs !
A model at once of oppreſſion and kindneſs.

Thy

Thy will, thou odd compound of goodnefs and whim,
Is a ftream, againft which it is treafon to fwim ;
Yet we muft crofs the current—

S E L I N A.

Dear Coufin, fay how !
Direct oppofition he will not allow :
What can you devife as a plan of prevention ?
How divert his keen fpirit from this new intention ?
I had much rather die than be ever united
To one of the lovers, that he has invited :
My heart has a thorough averfion to both :
Yet to make him unhappy I'm equally loth ;
When I think what I owe to his tender protection,
The worft of all ills is to lofe his affection.

M R s. F E L I X.

Dear Girl, your warm gratitude gives you new charms :
'Tis an amiable fear which your bofom alarms,
And I from your Uncle's quick humour would fcreen you,
Not loofen the bands of affection between you.
He merits your love, and you know he has mine ;
Yet we fomehow muft baffle his hafty defign,
Nor fuffer his whim thus to make you a wife,
To repent the rafh bufinefs the reft of his life.
Take courage ! kind chance may affift us—

S E L I N A.

SELINA.

I doubt it,

Yet Heaven knows how we fhall manage without it;
For when his heart's fet on a favourite fcheme,
His ardor and hafte, as you know, are extreme;
Like a med'cine ill-tim'd, oppofition is vain,
And inflames the diforder 'twas meant to reftrain.

MRS. FELIX.

In his fevers indeed there is no intermiffion;
And thanks gentle Coz! to your foft difpofition!
So fweet and compliant your temper has been,
You have taught him to think contradiction a fin;
And here all around him confirm that belief,
His vaffals all bow to the nod of their chief.
Here, fhut from the world in this rural dominion,
No mortal oppofes his will or opinion;
And thus he is fpoil'd—Politicians all fay,
Human nature's not fafhion'd for abfolute fway.

SELINA.

'Tis true, tho' the world, as you fay, think him odd,
In this fphere he is held a diminutive god:
And when I behold how his fortune is fpent,
In fuppreffing vexation, and fpreading content;

3

When

When I hear all the poor his kind bounty expreſſing,

And thoroughly know how he merits their bleſſing,

My feelings with theirs in his eulogy join,

And confeſs, that his nature is truly divine.

MRS. FELIX.

Thou excellent Girl! if ſuch fondneſs and zeal

For a warm-hearted, whimſical Uncle you feel,

With what fine ſenſations your boſom will glow,

What tender attachment your temper will ſhew,

When your fortunate lord Love and Hymen inveſt

With higher dominion o'er that gentle breaſt!

But tell me, dear Couſin—be honeſt—declare,

Has no young ſecret ſwain form'd an intereſt there?

I ſuſpeƈt—but don't let my ſuſpicion affright you,

Tho' the good Knight's rare virtues amuſe and de‐

       light you,

From this gloomy old hall you would wiſh to get free,

Had not Cupid preſerv'd you from feeling *ennui:*

Come tell me the name of the favourite youth;

I am ſure I gueſs right.

SELINA.

          No, in ſad ſober truth,

I never have ſeen, in the courſe of my life,

A mortal to whom I ſhould chuſe to be wife.

                    MRS.

Mrs. Felix.

Ye ftars, what a pity!—I wifh I could learn
That my Colonel from India would fhortly return,
Both for your fake and mine; for our prefent diftrefs
He would fpeedily turn into joyous fuccefs;
As his regiment muft fome young hero afford,
Who might throw at your feet both himfelf and his
    fword,
What fay you, my dear, to a foldier?—

Enter Jenny.

Jenny.

              Oh! Madam,
Here's young Mr. Sapphic— I vow, if I had them,
I'd give fifty pounds had you feen how politely
He begg'd me to tie a fweet nofegay up tightly,
Which is jolted to pieces.—Well, he's a fweet beau;
And now with his pencil he's writing below,
I believe 'tis a pofy he writes it fo neatly,
And I'm fure 'tis fine verfe, Ma'am, it founded fo
    fweetly.

Mrs. Felix.

Oh charming!—his vows will be very fublime,
And I truft we fhall hear his propofals in rhyme.

                        Selina.

SELINA.

How can you, dear Cousin, so cruelly jest in
A business you know I am really distrest in ?
I shall certainly forfeit my Uncle's protection,
For I never can wed where I feel no affection.
Do help me.

MRS. FELIX.

Good Girl, this perplexity smother,
And think your two lovers will banish each other :
There's much to be hop'd from our present affairs.

JENNY.

O, Ma'am, Mr. Sapphic is coming up stairs.

(*Aside as she goes out.*)

I am mightily pleas'd with this marrying plan,
And I hope in my spirit that he'll be the man.

[*Exit.*

Enter Sapphic.

SAPPHIC.

Fair Ladies, the moments have seem'd to be hours,
While I stopt in your hall to adjust a few flowers :
For the season, I'm told, they're uncommonly fine ;
But I still wish the tribute more worthy the shrine.

[*Bowing and presenting them to* Selina.

SELINA.

SELINA.

Mr. Sapphic is always extremely polite :
These roſes, indeed, are a wonderful ſight :
You are far better floriſts than we are.

MRS. FELIX.

My dear,

Mr. Sapphic has magic to make them appear,
And Flora is brib'd, by the ſongs he compoſes,
To produce for her poet extempore roſes ;
Into this early bloom all her plants are bewitch'd :
But you do not obſerve how the gift is inrich'd,
Here's a border of verſe, if my eyes don't deceive me.

SELINA, aſide to Mrs. Felix.

Dear Couſin, you'll read it—I pray you, relieve me ;
I ſhall bluſh like a fool at each civil expreſſion.

MRS. FELIX, aſide to Selina, taking the paper.

Now, with emphaſis juſt, and with proper diſcretion.

(Mrs. Felix reads.)

" Ye happy flowers, give and receive perfume
" As on Selina's fragrant breaſt ye bloom :
" From earth, tho' not arrang'd in order nice,
" Ye are tranſplanted into Paradiſe ;
" If on that ſpot ye languiſh into death,
" 'Twill be from envy of her ſweeter breath."

'Tis

'Tis a delicate compliment, tender and pretty,
What original fpirit! how graceful and witty!

SAPPHIC.

Dear Ma'am, you're too good, to find any thing in it,
'Tis a mere hafty trifle—the work of a minute:
On the anvil I had not a moment to hammer.
And I fear, in my hafte I have finn'd againft grammar.

MRS. FELIX.

All flight imperfections I never regard
When I meet with fuch vigor of thought in a bard,
With a fancy fo brilliant—

SAPPHIC.

O! Ma'am, you're too kind;
But candor's the teft of an amiable mind.
I wifh that your tafte all our Critics might guide,
To foften that rigor with which they decide.

MRS. FELIX.

From Critics, dear Sir, you have little to fear.
If Mr. Decifive himfelf had been here,
He muft have been charm'd with this fweet *jeu d'efprit,*
Which, as he is coming to-day, he fhall fee.
I am eager to hear how his wit will applaud it:
To conceal it would be of due praife to defraud it.

SAPPHIC.

SAPPHIC.

In Mercy's name, Ladies, I beg your protection,
Preferve my poor rhymes from Decifive's infpection;
Confider how hafty—

MRS. FELIX.

      Say rather how fprightly—

SAPPHIC.

Compos'd in a moment—

MRS. FELIX.

      Produc'd fo politely!

SAPPHIC.

He'll cut them to atoms!

MRS. FELIX.

      Dear Sir he's your friend,
And I thought he had feen all the poems you penn'd:
I was told that to him your long works you rehearfe—
Does Mr. Decifive himfelf write in verfe?

SAPPHIC.

I wifh from my foul that he did, now and then:
But he ufes the pen-knife much more than the pen,
And too freely has flafh'd all who write in the nation,
To give them an opening for retaliation.
My old friend Decifive has honour and wit;
To the latter, indeed, he makes moft things fubmit;

                     And

And thinks it fair sport, as a friend or a foe,
To knock down a Bard by a flaming *bon mot*.
To your sex indeed his chief failings I trace;
For the fair-ones so flatter'd his figure and face,
That too early he ceas'd the chaste Muses to follow,
And being Adonis, would not be Apollo.

MRS. FELIX.

Yet he has much fancy.

SAPPHIC.

O, Madam, no doubt,
And genius, that study would soon have brought out.
Had his thoughts been less turn'd to his legs and his
    looks,
Ere this he'd have written some excellent books:
'Tis pity such parts should thro' indolence fall;
But he never composes, and reads not at all.

SELINA.

Not read, Mr. Sapphic! you surely mistake;
Your friend cannot be an illiterate rake:
Our neighbours, who lately from London came down,
Declare, that his word forms the taste of the town.

SAPPHIC.

Dear Madam, the business is easily done;
He judges all authors, but never reads one.

MRS.

MRS. FELIX.

I'm fure he muſt own this *impromptu* is fweet,
And I vow he ſhall read it—

SAPPHIC.

Dear Ma'am, I intreat,
I conjure you to fpare me; this earneſt petition
I know you will grant me—

MRS. FELIX.

On this one condition,
That for fix lines fuppreſs'd you indulge me with twenty:
Come, ſhew us your pocket-book—there you have
plenty
Of tender poetical fquibs for the Fair.

SAPPHIC, *taking out his pocket-book.*
Dear Ma'am, here is nothing.

MRS. FELIX.

A volume, I fwear,
O, charming!—well, now you're an excellent man;
'Tis ſtuff'd like a pincuſhion—

SAPPHIC.

Yes, Ma'am— with bran.

MRS. FELIX.

Fie, fie, you're too modeſt, and murder my meaning;
What a harveſt is here! yet I aſk but a gleaning:

It would not be fair to feize all the collection,

Tho' all is moft certainly worthy infpection.

Indulge us, dear Sir : come, I'll take no refufal.

S A P P H I C.

Indeed, Ma'am, here's nothing that's fit for perufal.

M R s. F E L I X.

There are fifty fine things, and one can't chufe amifs.

S A P P H I C, *taking out a paper.*

Here's one new little fong—

M R s. F E L I X.

Well then, let me have this.

S A P P H I C, *after given a paper.*

They all are fo jumbled, I fear I am wrong;

I meant to have fhewn you a new little fong,

Which was written laft week on the ball at our

races,

Where I heard the Mifs Trotters compar'd to the

Graces ;

I could not help faying, 'twas very profane,

It was taking the name of the Graces in vain.

M R s. F E L I X *reads.*

" *On feeing Selina and Jenny near each other in*

" *the garden.*"

S A P P H I C.

SAPPHIC.

O mercy, dear Madam, you muſt not read thoſe !
A ſtanza unfiniſh'd.—

MRS. FELIX.

How ſweetly it flows !

Selina, pray hear it.

SELINA, *aſide to* MRS. FELIX.

Dear Couſin, enough !
How can you delight in his horrible ſtuff !

MRS. FELIX *reads.*

" Tho' each in the ſame garden blows,
    " The poet muſt be crazy,
" Who, when invited by the roſe,
    " Can ſtoop to pick the daiſy."

SELINA, *aſide to* MRS. FELIX.

If you love me, dear Couſin, aſſiſt me, I pray,
To end all this nonſenſe, and get him away.—
Pray, Sir, when you came, was my Uncle below ?

SAPPHIC.

He's abroad, Ma'am, your ſervant inform'd me—

SELINA.

O No !

You have heard he is building a temple to Pan,
And we hope that your taſte may embelliſh the plan :

O 2   At

At the end of the walk, in his favourite grove,
Where there formerly ſtood an old ruin'd alcove,
You'll find him ; and as 'tis an art you are ſkill'd in,
'Twill pleaſe him to know what you think of the building.

MRs. FELIX.

Ay do, Mr. Sapphic, inſpect what is done,
For the workmen all blunder'd when firſt they begun :
Your opinion, I'm ſure, will oblige the good Knight.

SELINA.

An inſcription, he once ſaid, he wiſh'd you to write.

SAPPHIC.

Dear Madam !—the hint is delightful, I vow;
To the God of Arcadia I haſten to bow:
I ſhall find the good Knight in the midſt of the dome ;
I am heartily glad that he is not from home.
We ſhall ſurely contrive ſomething clever between us,
And the Muſe will compoſe by the order of Venus.

[Bows tenderly to Selina, and Exit.

SELINA.

How could you ſo praiſe that impertinent creature ?
And praiſe him without diſcompoſing a feature !—
I could not have thought, before this converſation,
That your frankneſs could turn into ſuch adulation.

MRs.

MRS. FELIX:

The world, my dear Child, is to you quite unknown;
When you see it, you'll find such discourse is the *ton*;
Fine folks in high life learn to praise with great glee
Such persons and things as they sicken to see.
To me your best thanks for my speeches are due—
By thus flattering the Poet, I surely serve you;
He will now play the Sky-lark instead of the Dove,
And stún me with songs, while you're sav'd from his
    love.

Enter Jenny.

JENNY.

Dear Ma'am, now I hope Mr. Sapphic's quite blest,
For he flies thro' the walks like a bird to his nest.—
He's a sweet pretty gentleman.

MRS. FELIX, *aside to* Selina.

                 This, if I shew it,
Will soon banish Jenny's regard for the poet:—
Jenny, see what your friend Mr. Sapphic has written.

JENNY.

Dear Ma'am, with his verses I always am smitten.

(*Having read the stanza.*)

A Daisy indeed! to be sure I am neat,
But tho' I'm a servant, I hope I am sweet.

         O 3   When

When he makes my young Miſtreſs a Roſe or a Lily,
He might turn me at leaſt to a Daffy-down-dilly. .
But a Daiſy, forſooth ! with no fragrance at all !—
I'll croſs him for this—

SELINA.

What's that noiſe in the hall ?

JENNY.

As ſure as I live 'tis your other gay Spark,
For I ſaw a new chaiſe driving into the park.—
I'll ſee, Ma'am,

(Aſide going out.)

I'll ſhew this fine Poet a trick—
A Daiſy ! that no one but children will pick,   [Exit.

MRS. FELIX.

This ſimile Jenny I ſee cannot ſwallow,
And her anger may ruin this ſon of Apollo;
For in courtſhip this maxim is often diſplay'd,
He has half loſt the Miſtreſs who loſes the Maid.

Enter Deciſive.

DECISIVE.

Alone, my dear Ladies !— they told me below,
Our friend Sapphic was here, your poetical Beau ;
I was almoſt afraid that my ſudden intruſion
Might check the rich ſtream of ſome lyric effuſion.

(To

(*To* Selina.)

I am happy to see you so lovely to-day;
But I hope I've not frighted your Poet away.

SELINA.

O no—Mr. Sapphic had bid us adieu—

MRS. FELIX.

And not without saying some fine things of you:
He declares, that with those brilliant parts you possess,
'Tis a sin you ne'er send any work to the press.

DECISIVE.

Good Sapphic!—In truth 'tis his comfort to think
The whole duty of man lies in spilling of ink;
And at Paradise gate his large volumes of metre
Will, I hope, be allow'd a fair pass by Saint Peter.

MRS. FELIX.

Then the Saint must be free from your critical spirit,
For I know you have little esteem for their merit;
You're a rigorous judge, and to poets terrific.

DECISIVE.

I wish my friend's Muse was not quite so prolific:
But in rhymes, when a child, I have heard he would
    squeak;
And so proved a poet before he could speak;

O 4   On

On his death-bed, I doubt not, he'll ftill think of verfe,
And groan out a rhyme to his doctor or nurfe.

MRS. FELIX.

I fancy your favourite reading is profe;
Here's a new fet of travels, pray have you read thofe?

DECISIVE, *taking the book.*

This author is lucky to meet with a buyer;
A traveller's but a foft word for a liar.
Such works may pleafe thofe who have ne'er been
  abroad,
But men, who have travell'd, perceive all the fraud.

MRS. FELIX.

Is the work fo deceitful! it feems you have read it?

DECISIVE.

Not a fyllable, Madam—

MRS. FELIX.

   Pray who then has faid it?

DECISIVE.

Not a foul that I know—but fuch books are a trade,
And I perfectly know how thofe volumes are made.

MRS. FELIX.

'Tis a work, I am told, that has great reputation
Both for wit and for truth—

DECISIVE.

DECISIVE.

    We're a credulous nation—

MRS. FELIX.

Pray what kind of books are your favourite ſtudy?

DECISIVE.

I find modern works only make the brain muddy,
As my friends grew by reading more awkward than wiſe,
And ruin'd their perſons and clouded their eyes ;
I have wiſely reſolv'd not to read any more,
Since each living author is turn'd to a *bore*.

MRS. FELIX.

How can you ſo waſte all your bright mental powers?
'Tis pity you men have not ſuch works as ours—
What d'ye ſay to my knotting ?

                (*Takes out her work.*)

DECISIVE.

    Your box wants a hinge.
And I'll give you a much better pattern for fringe ;
I brought it from France.

MRS. FELIX.

    Now I ſee, my good friend,
There is no kind of work which your ſkill cannot
    mend ;

                    In

In all arts you poſſeſs a diſtinguiſhing head,
From building a temple to knotting a thread.

DECISIVE.

A-propos of a temple—pray has the good Knight
Rais'd his altar to Pan ?—he had fix'd on the ſite.
Is the ſtructure begun ?—I have not ſeen his plan—

MRS. FELIX.

Then haſten, and pay your devotions to Pan.
Sir Nicholas now in his veſtibule ſtands,
To guide all his workmen, and quicken their hands ;
And Sapphic is gone to attend the good Knight,
And try what inſcription his genius can write.

DECISIVE.

Poor Pan ! by the Graces thou'rt left in the lurch ;
Thy temple will look like a trim pariſh church,
With Sapphic's inſcriptions, like ſcraps of the Bible,
Put up, as the Church-wardens ſay, in a *libel*.

MRS. FELIX.

Indeed we much fear ſo—pray haſte to inſpect it,
And exert all your exquiſite taſte to correct it.

DECISIVE.

Ma'am I'll do what I can, for it puts me in wrath
To ſee a fine temple diſgrac'd by a Goth.   [*Exit.*

MRS.

MRs. FELIX.

Well, my dear, your two Lovers, like true men of
    fashion,
Do not pester you much with the heat of their passion,
You'll be quite at your ease—thanks to Pan and the
    Muse !

Enter Jenny, *hastily.*

JENNY.

News ! news ! my dear Ladies, most excellent news !

SELINA.

The girl is quite wild !

MRS. FELIX.

      What transports you so, Jenny ?

JENNY.

I've news for you, Madam, that's well worth a guinea :
I have news from the Colonel—

MRS. FELIX.

      A letter ! Where is it ?

JENNY.

No, Ma'am, here's a stranger arriv'd on a visit,
And he comes from the place where the Colonel is
    fighting.

MRS. FELIX.

And with letters for me ?

              JENNY.

JENNY.

   Madam, that I'm not right in ;
For, I run from his man when I got half my ſtory ;
But the Colonel, he ſays, is all riches and glory.

   MRS. FELIX.

Dear girl ! that's enough ; through my life I ſhall feel
Due regard for thy warm and affectionate zeal.
But where is this Stranger ?

   JENNY.

    Juſt walk'd to my Maſter.
His poor man has met with a cruel diſaſter ;
He was wounded in battle.

   SELINA.

    Pray treat him with care.——
In your joy, my dear Couſin, I heartily ſhare.

   MRS. FELIX.

This Stranger's a jewel for you from the Eaſt ;
He's a Captain, I hope, my dear Jenny, at leaſt.

   JENNY.

Ah, Madam ! my fancy ſuppos'd him ſo too ;
But we're both in the wrong, and for Miſs he won't do,
For I learnt from his man he is only a Doctor.

   MRS. FELIX.

Poor Jane ! how the difference of title has ſhock'd her !
          For

For my part I can't find, by my reaſon or feeling,
That the art of deſtroying excels that of healing:
We may equally love the profeſſors of both.

JENNY.

That Miſs tho' ſhould marry a Doctor, I'm loth.

MRS. FELIX.

Come, my dear, let us meet 'em—I can't reſt above—
How ſlowly fly letters from hands that we love!

End of ACT I.

❋❋❋❋❋❋❋❋❋❋❋❋❋❋❋❋❋❋❋❋❋❋❋❋❋❋❋❋❋❋

ACT II.

SCENE I.

Enter Jenny *and* Jonathan.

JENNY.

COME, dear Mr. Jonathan, tell me the whole:
 An account of a battle I love to my ſoul;
There is nothing on earth I ſo truly delight in,
As to hear a brave Soldier diſcourſe about fighting.—
So the Colonel was wounded, you ſay, near the wall:
Whereabouts was the ſhot? Did he inſtantly fall?

JONATHAN.

JONATHAN.

No; recoiling a little, he rush'd on again,
And fought like a lion, made fiercer by pain;
Tho' a curfed keen arrow, an Indian let fly,
Pierc'd the bone of his cheek juft below the right eye.
'Twas a horrible wound! but it could not appall him.

JENNY.

O mercy! that fuch a hard fate fhould befall him.
Alas! I'm afraid that his fine manly face
Muft have loft by the fcar all its fpirit and grace.
Does he look very hideous?

JONATHAN.

No; thanks to my Mafter,
You can hardly perceive that he e'er wore a plaifter.
There never was known a more wonderful cure;
But kind Heaven affifts my good Mafter, I'm fure;
Without it, the fkill of no mortal could fave
The many brave lads he has kept from the grave.
You would weep with delight to behold him furrounded
With a hundred fine fellows, once horribly wounded;
Who with thanks for their lives are ftill eager to
        greet him,
And hail him with bleffings whenever they meet him.

7   JENNY.

JENNY.

God reward him, fay I, for the good he has done ;
And of thofe he has fav'd I'm glad you are one.

JONATHAN.

Aye, twice he preferv'd me when all thought me dead,
And once brought me off at the rifque of his head.
It was not his bufinefs to mix in the ftrife,
And fome thought him mad when he ventur'd his life
'To bring off a poor mangled private like me ;
But I've ftill a heart left, in this trunk that you fee,
Which loves the brave fpirit who fnatch'd me from
      death,
And will ferve him, I hope, till my very laft breath.

JENNY.

Your fcenes of hard fervice, I hope, are all over ;
It is now fairly time you fhould both live in clover.
Your Mafter, I truft, has brought home as much
      treafure
As will make him a parliament-man at his pleafure ;
And, to recompenfe you for the wound in your arm,
Perhaps he will buy you a fnug little farm.

JONATHAN.

When a Gentleman comes from the Eaft, my good girl,
You all think he is loaded with diamonds and pearl ;

You

You fancy his treafure too great to be told,
And fuppofe he poffeffes a mountain of gold.
A few daring blades, by a bold kind of ftealth,
Have indeed from the Indies brought home fo much
      wealth,
That with all their keen fenfes they ne'er could em-
      ploy it,
And have dy'd from the want of a heart to enjoy it:
But fome hundred brave lads, whom gay youth led to
      enter
That promifing region of hope and adventure,
Have toil'd many years in thofe rich burning climes,
With fmall fhare of their wealth, and with none of
      their crimes.
Now my Mafter and I both belong to this tribe;
Not a fingle Nabob have we kill'd for a bribe;
And to tell you a truth, which I hope you'll not
      doubt,
We're as poor and as honeft as when we fet out.

JENNY.

What! your Mafter ftill poor in fo thriving a trade!
And, with patients fo rich, has he never been paid
For the wounds he has heal'd?

JONATHAN,

JONATHAN.

    Yes, my dear, for his fees
I know he has touch'd many thousand rupees;
But the sight of distress he could never endure;
What he took from the rich he bestow'd on the poor.

JENNY.

Well, Heaven will pay him, no doubt, in due season.
But what brings him home?—I would fain know the
  reason
Why he leaves that rich land in the bloom of his life:
I suppose, from the want of a cherry-check'd wife?
They say those black wenches are sad nasty creatures,
And tho' they've fine shapes they have horrible features.
Does he want a white sweetheart? or has he a Black?

JONATHAN.

'Tis indeed a white woman that brings us both back:
But, alas! 'tis an old one—my Master, it seems,
Has a fond simple mother that's troubled with dreams,
And he, like a tender and soft-hearted youth,
Resigns his fine prospect, and comes home, forsooth,
Because the old dame has exprefs'd her desires
To see him in England before she expires:
And egad, since he's come she will live long enough,
For she seems to be made of good durable stuff.

JENNY.

Well, now I fhall love him a hundred times more
Than I did for the ftories you told me before.
God blefs the kind foul ! who behaves to his mother
As if he well knew he could ne'er have another ;
And were he my fon, I could not live without him ;
I could ftay here all day while you're talking about
   him.—

But 'tis time to be gone ; we muft both difappear,
For the Colonel's fweet Wife and your Mafter are here.

JONATHAN.

Stop, I muft peep at her;—fhe's as bright as the day !

JENNY.

And her heart is as good as her fpirit is gay—
Come I'll fhew you our walks—we may get out
   this way.   [*Exeunt.*

   Enter Mrs. Felix *and* Morley.

MRS. FELIX.

Dear excellent Friend, fince I owe to your worth
The fafety of what I moft value on earth,
With thofe it loves beft my heart yields you a place,
And I clafp your kind hand with a fifter's embrace.
To judge of the man whom fuch fervice endears,
I want not the tardy acquaintance of years ;

          But

But in ftrong tho' quick ties, that no chances can fever,
In an inftant he feizes my friendfhip for ever:
And had I much lefs obligation to you,
My regard and efteem I fhould ftill think your due,
From the picture my Felix has drawn of your mind.

MORLEY.

His warm foul to his friends is moft partially kind:
But fuch as I am I moft truly am yours;
Your goodnefs my grateful attachment enfures,
And my heart with proud tranfport your friendfhip
        embraces.
Tho' I ne'er gaz'd before on your perfonal graces,
I've beguil'd fome long weeks of hard wearifome duty
With frequent difcourfe on your virtues and beauty;
And I own for the Colonel it rais'd my efteem,
To mark with what pleafure he dwelt on the theme.

MRS. FELIX.

You're an excellent creature to footh a fond Wife,
Who regards her Lord's love hardly lefs than his life;
But fince you've replied with good-humour fo fteady
To the ten thoufand queftions I've afk'd you already,
I'll fpare you to-day, and, if 'tis in my power,
Mention Felix's name only once in an hour.

That

That my thoughts to the Indies no longer may roam,
Let me talk to you now about matters at home;
Your counfel may make our perplexity lefs,
And finifh our odd tragi-comic diftrefs.
Firft tell me, and fpeak without any difguife,
(Tho' I fancy I read all your thoughts in your eyes)
What d'ye think of my Coufin?

MORLEY.

Her graces indeed
The glowing defcription of Felix exceed;
Tho' in praifing her, oft he with pleafure has fmil'd,
Like a father defcribing his favourite child.
For my part, I think fhe is lavifhly bleft
With thofe beauties by which the pure mind is expreft,
That her heart is with truth and with tendernefs warm,
That fweet fenfibility fhines in her form;
A form, on which no man his eye ever turn'd
Without feeling his breaft in her welfare concern'd.
'Tis the lot of fuch graces, wherever they dwell,
None can fee their foft miftrefs and not wifh her well.

MRS. FELIX.

Very gallantly faid, and the praife is her due—
But how came her Lovers fo well known to you?

MORLEY.

MORLEY.

Her Lovers !—dear Madam, I hope you're in jeft—
Or if by their vows your fweet Friend is addreft,
Heaven grant, for the peace of her delicate mind,
That her hand may be never to either refign'd !

MRS. FELIX.

From my foul, I affure you, I join in your prayer;
But whence does it fpring?

MORLEY.

I will freely declare,
Tho' they're both men of fortune, fair birth, and good
  name,
With figures that fet fome young nymphs in a flame;
Tho' at each, many ladies are ready to catch
At what the world calls, a moft excellent match;
Yet, if I have read your fair Coufin aright,
A bofom fo tender, a fpirit fo bright,
Muft be wretched with fuch a companion for life,
As each of thefe Lovers would prove to his Wife.

MRS. FELIX.

You are right; but their characters where could you
  know?

MORLEY.

I knew them at college a few years ago,

Before,

Before, by a whimſical odd ſort of fate,
And ſome family loſſes, too long to relate,
In Europe my views of proſperity ceas'd,
And chance ſent me forth to my friends in the Eaſt.

MRS. FELIX.

Pray what ſort of youths were thoſe two modiſh men?

MORLEY.

You now find them both what they ſeem'd to me then;
Two characters form'd like moſt young men of faſhion,
Whoſe cold ſelfiſh pride is their ſovereign paſſion:
In each, tho' they're men of an oppoſite turn,
The ſame heart-freezing vanity ſtill you diſcern.
To indulge that dear vanity, each ſtill diſplays
All the force of his mind, tho' in different ways.
Thence, in ſpinning weak verſe Sapphic's toil never
    ends,
And Deciſive ne'er ſtops in deriding his friends;
Each equally fancies no nymph can reſiſt
His lips, which he thinks all the Graces have kiſt.

MRS. FELIX.

Perfect knowledge of both your juſt picture has
    ſhown!—
The warmth of theſe Lovers diverts me, I own.

Of

Of conqueſt each ſeems to himſelf very clear,
And feels from his rivals no diffident fear.
'Tis eaſy to ſee, from their ſatisfied air,
Each loves his own perſon much more than the Fair.
But, my poor gentle Coz wiſhes both at a diſtance ;
And I want to contrive, by your friendly affiſtance,
To relieve her, and quietly ſend them from hence
Without the Knight's knowledge.

MORLEY.

                        As neither wants ſenſe,
Can't the Lady pronounce their diſiniſſion at once,
Which none can miſtake but an impudent dunce ?

MRS. FELIX.

This meaſure ſeems eaſy indeed at firſt view ;
But, alas ! 'tis a meaſure we dare not purſue.
Our warm-hearted, whimſical, poſitive Knight,
Allows not to woman this natural right ;
And hence my young Friend, in a pitiful caſe,
Knows not how to rejeſt what ſhe ne'er can embrace ;
For nothing her Uncle's reſentment could ſmother,
Should ſhe baniſh one ſuitor, and not take the other.

MORLEY.

Then indeed I am griev'd for the Lady's diſtreſs ;
But how can I aid her ?

P 4   MRS.

Mrs. Felix.

'Tis hard, I confefs,
To a fudden retreat this bold Pair to oblige,
And make two fuch Heroes abandon a fiege;
Yet I wifh we could do it—and when they recede,
The departure of both muft appear their own deed.

Morley, *after a paufe.*

Well—my friendfhip for you has fuggefted a fcheme.

Mrs. Felix.

'Tis a fervice our hearts will for ever efteem,
But what is your project?

Morley.

Don't queftion me what,
Left you think me a fool for too fimple a plot:
'Tis fimple, and yet I would venture my life
It will drive from thefe Beaus all their thoughts of a Wife;
And if my fcheme profpers, with joy I'll confefs
What a whimfical trifle produc'd our fuccefs.

Mrs. Felix.

Well, keep your own fecret, if filence is beft;
Tho' a woman, for once I'll in ignorance reft.—
Here comes our friend Sapphic—he feems in a flurry.

Morley.

His ftep fhews indeed a poetical hurry,

And

And we shall be call'd in as Gossips, fair neighbour,
For by the Bard's bustle his Muse is in labour.

Enter Sapphic.

S A P P H I C.

Dear Ma'am ! may I ask you for paper and ink,
Lest a fresh *jeu d'esprit* in oblivion should sink ?
For when my free fancy has brought forth my verse,
My treacherous memory proves a bad nurse.

M R S. F E L I X.

O pray ! for your Muse let us rear her young chit,
For the bantling, no doubt, must have spirit and wit ;
As a cradle to hold it I beg you'll take that,

(giving him a paper.)

And your Friend here will aid you in dressing the Brat ;
At a rite so important I merit no place,
And I beg to withdraw while you're washing its face.

[*Exit.*

S A P P H I C.

That's a charming gay creature—luxuriant and young—
But I've lost half a stanza—the deuce take her tongue ;—
Let me see—let me see if I can't recollect it—
'Tis done ;—and now, Morley, pray hear or inspect it.

M O R L E Y.

The Poet himself his own verse should recite.

S A P P H I C.

SAPPHIC.

You're a fenfible fellow—your maxim is right.

(*Reads.*)

" Thy old Arcadia, Pan, refign,
 " For this more rich retreat :
" A fairer nymph here decks thy fhrine ;
 " Be this thy fav'rite feat."

Well, my Friend, won't this bring the old God out of

Greece ?

MORLEY.

Aye, and make good Sir Nicholas give you his Niece.

SAPPHIC.

Yes, I fancy this ftanza will make the Girl mine.

MORLEY.

What Poet can wifh for a prize more divine ?
I give you much joy on your conqueft, my Friend ;
Yet the eyes of regret on your nuptials I bend,
And grieve in reflecting, that conjugal joy
Your poetical harveft of Fame muft deftroy.

SAPPHIC.

What the deuce do you mean ?

MORLEY.

To thofe great works
Which the world now expects with impatience from you.

The

'The Poet when bleſt can no more be ſublime,
And a chill matrimonial muſt ſtrike thro' his rhyme.

S A P P H I C.

You're miſtaken, dear Doctor—connubial delight
Will give a new zeſt to each poem I write ;
And you'll ſee ſuch productions !—

M o r l e y.

'Tis true, now and then
Polemics by marriage have quicken'd their pen.
A Dutch Critic, I know, by the aid of his Wife,
Made a book and a child every year of his life.
But total ſecluſion from Venus and Bacchus,
Is, you know, to the Bard recommended by Flaccus.
A grand epic poem I hear you are writing ;
'Tis a work that your country will take great de-
        light in :
But conſider, my Friend, when you're deep in heroics,
As Poets have not all the patience of Stoics,
How you'll grieve to be check'd in the flow of your
        verſe,
By a young ſqualling child and an old ſcolding nurſe ;
E'en the qualms of your Lady may drive from your
        brain
Fine thoughts that you ne'er can recover again ;

Reflect

Reflect how you'll feel, with such hopes of succeeding,
If your Muse should miscarry because your Wife's
     breeding.

S A P P H I C.

Egad, in that case I should think my fate hard.

M O R L E Y.

I myself have beheld an unfortunate Bard,
Who his nails for a rhyme unsuccefsfully bit,
When family cares had extinguifh'd his wit.—
With many who fing in the Mufe's full choir,
It would do them no mifchief to muffle their lyre;
But for you, whom the Nine, with tender prefage,
Are prepar'd to proclaim the firft Bard of our age;
For you, who of Tafte are the favourite theme—

S A P P H I C.

Yes, I think I ftand high in the public efteem.

M O R L E Y.

For you, I fhould grieve if domeftic delight
On your fair rifing laurels fhould fall as a blight.
'Tis the pride of great minds, whom the Mufes inflame,
To facrifice joy on the altar of Fame:
Your paffion's renown—of this Girl are you fonder?—
On this delicate point I muft leave you to ponder;
Confider it, while I attend the old Knight.   [Exit.

S A P P H I C.

SAPPHIC, *alone (after a pause.)*

By Jove, I believe my friend Morley is right.

Thou, Fame, art my Miſtreſs ; to win thee I ſing.

This Girl, tho' ſhe's handſome, is but a dull thing.

'Tis clear, whenſoe'er I a poem rehearſe,

That ſhe has no reliſh for elegant verſe.——

Her fortune indeed would be rather convenient,

But the glorious, to me, is before the expedient.

Egad, I'd quit Venus herſelf, if I knew

That the ſyſtem of Morley was certainly true.

I don't think the Girl to Deciſive inclin'd ;

But here comes her Maid, who may tell me her mind.

Enter Jenny.

My good little Jenny, you're truſty and true,

And your Miſtreſs, I know, tells her ſecrets to you.

What you know, to a friend you may ſafely impart,

And give me a perfect account of her heart :

Pray how do I ſtand in your Lady's regard ?

JENNY.

Now's my time to be even with this ſaucy Bard.

(aſide.)

To be ſure, Sir, the taſte of my Lady is odd ;

But poetry moves her no more than a clod.

SAPPHIC.

SAPPHIC.

What! no relifh for rhyme!—Does fhe never repeat
The foft little fonnets I've laid at her feet?

JENNY.

Ah, Sir! would my Miftrefs were once of my mind,
(For I read all the verfes of yours that I find);
But my Lady's fo cruel fhe thwarts my defire,
And to hide them from me throws them into the fire.

SAPPHIC.

She's a fool—fhe's a fool *(afide.)*—I fhould have a
        fine life,
With fuch a profaic dull jade of a wife.

JENNY.

But, my good Sir, I hope you will not be dejected,
I could tell you by whom all your wit is refpected.
There's a heart upon which you have made fuch im-
        preffion—
But I muft not betray her by my indifcretion.

SAPPHIC.

Whom d'ye mean, my good Jenny? come, tell me,
        my dear.

JENNY.

You would make a bad ufe of the fecret, I fear.—

9   Now

Now I hope I ſhall lead the Bard into a ſcrape, *(aſide.)*
For he bites like a Gudgeon, and cannot eſcape.

S A P P H I C.

Come, ſay who's in love with me—if ſhe is fair,
I'll not leave the dear creature, I vow, to deſpair.

J E N N Y.

O lud ! I proteſt ſhe is coming this way ;
But I did not intend her regard to betray.
I muſt fly—but I beg that you'll not be too free.

[Exit.

S A P P H I C.

Madam Felix !—I thought ſhe was partial to me.

Enter Mrs. Felix.

M R s. F E L I X.

May I enter without incommoding the Muſe ?

S A P P H I C.

By a queſtion like this your own charms you abuſe.
Thoſe eyes, my dear Madam, were form'd, I profeſs,
To inſpirit a Poet, and not to depreſs ;
From your preſence he ſurely muſt catch inſpiration.

M R s. F E L I X.

A very poetical fine ſalutation !
But I ſeriouſly beg, if you're buſy with rhyme,
That you will not allow me to take up your time.

As

As I'm not Selina, you're free from reſtriction,
And may tell me plain truths, unembelliſh'd with fiction.

SAPPHIC.

Then I ſwear, my dear creature, I ſwear by this hand,
That I feel as I touch it my genius expand ;
That your lips—O by Jove ! he's a madman or booby,
Who roves to the Indies for diamond or ruby ;
And each vein in my heart his ſtrange folly condemns,
Who leaves theſe more bright and more exquiſite gems.
Sweet Fair ! let me keep, while their richneſs I praiſe,
The cold damp of neglect from o'erclouding their rays.

(*While* Mr. Sapphic *kiſſes* Mrs. Felix *with great*
vehemence, Jenny *enters unperceived.*)

JENNY.

O ho !—have I caught you ? impertinent Poet !
This is more than I hop'd for—my Maſter ſhall know
it.   [*Exit.*

MRS. FELIX.

Good God ! Mr. Sapphic, what frantic illuſion
Has produc'd this ridiculous ſcene of confuſion ?
All Poets are Quixotes in love, I am told ;
And the truth of the adage in you I behold.
As the Knight once miſtook an old mill for a giant,
Your ſenſe as diſorder'd, your fancy as pliant,

Takes

Takes me for my Coufin—your love's ebullition
I only can pardon on this fuppofition.
I fain would fuppofe that no infult was meant,
Nor believe you could think, what I ought to refent.

SAPPHIC.

O! talk not of anger, with lips that infpire
The ftrongeft fenfation of rapturous fire,
That with love's fweet convulfions fhake every nerve;
O! think not that I your refentment deferve;
Becaufe my warm heart, thus engrofs'd by your
     charms;
Is ambitious of filling thefe dear empty arms.
No, let me, while bafking beneath your bright eye,
The place of a thanklefs deferter fupply;
And in this melting breaft kindle ecftacy's flame,
Which Nature defign'd for fo glowing a frame.

MRS. FELIX.

Away, Sir!—and fince in your fondling infanity
You reject the excufe which I form'd for your vanity,
My threats muft inform you—

SAPPHIC.

      O! frown not, fweet creature;
Let not wrath fpoil the charm of thy every feature.

Mrs. Felix.

Regain you your fenfe—from my wrath you are free,
Which fhould not be rais'd by a being like thee;
Begone then!—my pardon in vain you'll implore,
If you dare on this fubject to breathe a word more.

Sapphic.

Words, indeed, my warm fair one, by Nature's con-
    feffion,
For the love that I feel are no proper expreffion;
The foul's fond intent in foft murmurs fhould fwell,
And kiffes explain what no language can tell.
Ye Gods, how luxuriant!

Mrs. Felix.

            Away! quit my arm!
Or my cries in an inftant the houfe fhall alarm.

Sapphic.

Provoking fweet creature!—indulge my fond paffion;
Come, come, don't I know you're a woman of fafhion?
Your coynefs, I've heard, you can fometimes give
    over;
And I'm fure you're too wife to be true to a rover.
Befides, I have learnt, that with partial regard
You have caft a kind eye on your ill-treated Bard.

Mrs. Felix.

Away! thou vain coxcomb! nor, bafe as thou art,
Infult the bright Lord of fo loyal a heart;
Begone!— I abhor thee—my perfon releafe!—

Sir Nicholas, *entering.*

Is it thus, my young Sir, you pay court to my Niece?

Sapphic.

Confufion! What devil has fent the old Knight?

Sir Nicholas.

How dare you, pert ftripling, almoft in my fight·
To infult a chafte female that's under my roof?—
But fince of your bafenefs you give me fuch proof,
You fhall feel it repaid by a proper correction.

Sapphic (*afide.*)

Deuce take this perverfe and unlucky detection:
I wifh I had wifely, as Morley had taught me,
Renounc'd that jade Venus before he thus caught me.
What excufe can I make him?——(*To* Sir Nicho-
    las) My dear worthy Sir,
Tho' I now feem moft juftly your wrath to incur,
Yet as you grow cool, your opinion will vary,
You will not refent fuch an idle vagary,
A mere romping frolic—

SIR NICHOLAS.

A frolic, d'ye fay!

Then a frolic of mine fhall your frolic repay.—
Call our fervants to punifh this frolicfome fpark,
They fhall drag him acrofs the new pond in the park.

SAPPHIC *(afide.)*

'Tis what he can't mean—yet his countenance fuch is,
I wifh from my foul I was out of his clutches.—

(To Sir Nicholas.)

Dear Sir, I affure you, I'm griev'd beyond meafure
That I thus have awaken'd your furious difpleafure;
When calmer—

SIR NICHOLAS.

Young man, I am not in a fury,
A fentence more juft never came from a jury;
Such frolics as yours have Old England difgrac'd:
In high life let them flourifh as fafhion and tafte.
To thofe wanton young fellows I am not fevere,
Who attack the loofe Wife of a vain gambling Peer.
My Lady, whofe Lord waftes at Hazard the night,
May plead to more generous pleafures fome right;
I care not how each keeps their conjugal oath,
Since honour and peace muft be ftrangers to both.

But

But when a brave Soldier, pure Glory's true fon,
Ennobled with laurels laborioufly won ;
When rifking in far diftant climates his life,
To his Country he leaves a fair innocent Wife ;
Accurft be the man, who to friendfhip unjuft,
Fails to guard as his foul this moft delicate truft ;
Or to punifh thofe fops who infult her chafte beauty,
And invite her to fwerve from her honour and duty.
Of the doom that I think to fuch libertines due,
I will give to the world an example in you.
Our old Englifh difcipline, Ducking, by name,
Shall atone for your outrage, by quenching your flame.
Here ! William and John—

MRS. FELIX.

       For my fake, I intreat
That you will not, dear Sir, this rough-vengeance
  compleat.

SIR NICHOLAS.

By Jupiter, Coufin, to make him lefs fond,
He fhall croak out his love to the frogs of our
  pond.—
Here, William ! tell Jack after Stephen to fkip,
And tell the old Huntfman to come with his whip,

Q 3

         Then

Then wait all together around the hall door.

SAPPHIC.

O mercy, dear Sir ! I your mercy implore.
You will not deſtroy me ?

SIR NICHOLAS.

No, only correct,
And teach you a brave Soldier's Wife to reſpect.

MRS. FELIX.

Yet think, my dear Couſin, yet think, for my ſake,
What a noiſe this ridiculous matter will make.
You know that my Felix's nature is ſuch,
He don't wiſh his Wife to be talk'd of too much ;
His honour and quiet let us make our care,
And bury in ſilence this fooliſh affair :
Perhaps, in my manners too eaſy and gay,
My levity led the young Poet aſtray.

SIR NICHOLAS.

No, no ! my good creature, you muſt not arraign
Your innocent ſelf in a buſineſs ſo plain :
Beſides, his offence by this plea cannot ſink,
For they are the worſt of all puppies that think
Each woman's a wanton who is not preciſe,
And that cheerfulneſs muſt be the herald of vice.

MRS.

Mrs. Felix.

Howe'er this may be—as he's now all repentance,
I earneftly beg a repeal of your fentence.

Sapphic.

Dear Ma'am I adore you for this intercefsion ;
And I truft the good Knight will forgive my tranf-
 grefsion.

Sir Nicholas.

Well, Sir, as beyond your defert you're befriended
By that virtue which you have fo grofsly offended,
You are free to depart ; but remember, young fwain,
That you ne'er touch the Wife of a Soldier again.

Sapphic.

If I do, may I die by the wind of a ball !
Heaven blefs you, good folks, and this fociable hall !
Since my amorous folly your friendfhip thus lofes,
My amours fhall henceforth be confin'd to the Mufes.

                                                    [*Exit.*

Mrs. Felix.

I thank you, dear Sir, and rejoice in my heart
That in fafety you've fuffer'd this youth to depart.

Sir Nicholas.

By Jupiter, Coz, I had cool'd your warm Poet,
Had I not been afraid all our neighbours might know it,

And make you the fubject of fuch converfation
As I think your nice Colonel would hear with vexa-
tion.
Then, fince for your fake I have let the Bard go,
Come and aid me to fettle all matters below:
That my anxious cares in her comfort may ceafe,
I'm refolv'd young Decifive fhall marry my Niece.

End of A C T II.

A C T III.

S C E N E I.

Enter Mrs. Felix *and* Selina.

MRS. FELIX.

WELL, my dear, what d'ye think of our me-
dical friend,
Whom the letters of Felix fo highly commend?
If my gratitude does not my judgment miflead,
He's the man in the world who with you might fuc-
ceed;

The'

Tho' gentle, yet manly, tho' bafhful, polite.
Are you not half in love ?—

SELINA.

     Yes, indeed, at firft fight !—
His fervice to you on my heart is engrav'd,
And I love him, I own, for the life he has fav'd.
To win me perhaps he might not find it hard,
So efteem'd as he is by the friends I regard;
But I fancy fuch thoughts will not enter his brain:
And for my part, inftead of attracting a fwain,
I only fhall think, as they heartily vex me,
Of efcaping from thofe who already perplex me.

MRS. FELIX.

O make yourfelf eafy, I pray, on that head;
In the deepeft difgrace the poor Poet is fled,
And I truft that the Critic will foon fhare his fate.
Come with me—I've a moft curious tale to relate.
Let us hafte—I perceive that Decifive is near,
In whofe prefent difcourfe I would not interfere.

          [*Exeunt.*

Enter Decifive *and* Morley.

DECISIVE.

So while in the grove I was cooly projecting
New plans for the temple the Knight is erecting,

        Our

Our Poet, addicted to amorous fin,
Grew a little too fond of the Ladies within:
But difcovery happen'd his paffion to damp;
And this is the caufe of his hafte to decamp.

MORLEY.

The old Knight, I believe, fuch refentment exprefs'd
As quicken'd the fpeed of his fugitive gueft;
On Terror's fwift wing he is certainly flown,
And as he has retreated, the field is your own.

DECISIVE.

As a rival I had not much fear of poor Sapphic;
Bad rhyme's current coin in moft amorous traffic,
But would not pafs here.

MORLEY.

     I think not in your view,
As it finds fuch a critical touchftone in you.
The Poet's difmiffion your triumph enfures,
And the prize, my good friend, is now certainly yours;
A prize, that we juftly may call very great,
A lovely fweet girl with a noble eftate.

DECISIVE.

The girl's very well, but knows nothing of life;
It will coft me fome pains to new model my Wife;

8

But

But I think fhe will gladly receive my correction,
And my wealthy old kinfman approves the connection.

(Coughs.)

M o r l e y.

You've a cough, my good friend.

D e c i s i v e.

Yes, a trifling one : Hem !

Have you got any Indian prefcription for phlegm ?

M o r l e y.

Believe me, that cough is no trifling affair ;
It calls, I affure you, for caution and care.
With regret I point out fo unpleafant a truth,
But your conftitution I've known from your youth ;
Your hectic appearance I fee with concern,
As I know, with your frame, if health takes fuch a turn,
The leaft indifcretion your life may deftroy.
The flighteft excefs in diverfion and joy ;
Even thofe tender cares, which on life's pureft plan
Muft belong to the ftate of a Family Man,
May lead to difeafe from which art cannot fave,
And rapidly hurry you into the grave.
'T'were better this courtfhip of yours fhould mifcarry,
For you'll certainly die in fix months if you marry.

D e c i s i v e.

DECISIVE.

Are you ferious, dear Doctor?

MORLEY.

By fuch a fad end
I lately have loft a poor good-humour'd friend.
You remember Jack Dangle at College, no doubt;
He was juft of your age, and a little more ftout;
He, with other young fages, left Weftminfter Hall
To teach Englifh law to the flaves of Bengal.
But Jack, in his new chamber-practice at leaft,
Too eagerly follow'd the rules of the Eaft.
A bad cough enfu'd, much like yours in its found—

(Decifive *coughs.*)

Good God! I could fwear 'twas poor Jack under
    ground,
'Tis his tone fo exactly, fepulchral and hollow!
The fyftem he flighted I hope you will follow.
With pains in his breaft he was fharply tormented;
But as he at firft to my guidance confented,
Some time my ftrict regimen kept him alive,
Poor Dangle once more was beginning to thrive;
And had he fome months in my plan perfever'd,
On the earth at this moment he might have appear'd;

But

But chance threw a pretty white girl in his way,

And eager for marriage, fond Jack would not ftay:

In vain I conjur'd him to wait half a year,

And fhew'd him the danger he ran very clear.

He thought the remains of his cough but a trifle,

And, being unable his paffion to ftifle,

He took his fair wife ;—but, alas ! the vile cough

Encreas'd every day till it carried him off !

DECISIVE.

I don't recollect any pain in my breaft,

But I feel a ftrange tightnefs juft now in my cheft.

MORLEY.

How's your ftomach ?

DECISIVE.

I've nothing to fear on that fcore.

MORLEY.

Do you eat as you did ?

DECISIVE.

Yes, I think rather more,

MORLEY.

That ravenous hunger's the thing that I dread.

How d'ye fleep ?

DECISIVE.

All the time that I pafs in my bed.

MORLEY.

MORLEY.

Indeed?—I don't like fo lethargic a flumber.

DECISIVE.

Why! my friend! of good fymptoms thefe rank in
the number.

MORLEY.

Alas! you may call them all good if you pleafe,
By that title you only confirm your difeafe,
In which tho' the patient declines very faft,
He for ever will flatter himfelf to the laft,
Believe me, your fymptoms are rather alarming,
Yet your prefent diforder there is not much harm in,
If you can but abftain, with a fpirit refign'd,
From all that may harrafs your body or mind.
To a different climate I wifh you'd repair.
And for one winter breathe a lefs changeable air.
Spend a Chriftmas at Naples, and when you return
You may marry without any anxious concern.
But you're now at that critical period of life
When, in fuch frames as yours, nature feels an odd
  ftrife,
And, if quiet does not all her functions befriend,
The fhort earthly fcene on a fudden will end.
On a point fo important you'll pardon my freedom.

DECISIVE.

DECISIVE.

Your cautions oblige me, I feel that I need 'em,
For in truth I am growing as thin as a rabbit,
And there's something confumptive I know in my habit.
My father died foon after taking a wife,
And cough'd out his foul when I jump'd into life:
I fuppofe I am going.

MORLEY.

Take courage, my friend;
On your own prudent conduct your life will depend.
If you take but due care for two years, I'll engage
You will ftand a fair chance for a healthy old age.
Nor would I advife you this girl to refufe,
A diftant attachment your mind will amufe;
And, no doubt, for a man of your fortune and figure
She will wait till your health has recover'd its vigour.

DECISIVE.

I can part with the girl without feeling a chafm
In my heart; that will fhake with no amorous fpafm;
For, to tell you the truth, my old rich Uncle Cob
Is more eager than I for this marrying job.
By this fcheme the old blade is fupremely delighted,
Becaufe two large manors may thus be united:

But

But when of his park, I've extended the bound,
It will do me small good if I sink under ground ;
And I'm not such a fool, in these projects of pelf,
To humour my friends and endanger myself.

MORLEY.

Indeed I'd not wed for an old Uncle's whim ;—
But here comes our Knight, I shall leave you with him,
As I think you've some delicate points to adjust. [*Exit.*

DECISIVE, *alone.*

I'm in no haste to sleep with my Anceſtors' dust.
'Tis wiser my weak conſtitution to save,
Than to marry, and so travel post to the grave.

Enter Sir Nicholas.

SIR NICHOLAS.

Come, give me your hand, and rejoice, my young
 neighbour,
You're the man that's to order the pipe and the tabor ;
And by Jove we'll all dance on so joyous a day :
Your wedding, dear Dick, shall be speedy and gay ;
For your rival is gone with our serious diſpleaſure,
And I give to your wishes my young lovely treasure.
A treasure she is, tho' the girl is my niece ;
Heaven grant ye long years of affection and peace !

And

And a fine chopping boy ere the end of the firſt—
Remember that I am to ſee the rogue nurs'd.
Go, you happy young dog, go and ſeal with a kiſs,
And teach the old hall to re-echoe your bliſs.
As I know on this match what Sir Jacob intends,
And we can ſo well truſt each other as friends,
Short contracts will anſwer as well as the beſt,
Our lawyers at leiſure may finiſh the reſt.
I know all ſuſpence in ſuch caſes is hard,
And you ſhall not, I ſwear, from your bliſs be debarr'd,
While o'er acres of parchment they're crawling like
    ſnails.

DECISIVE.

Dear Sir, upon weighing in Reaſon's juſt ſcales
Your very great favours, and my weak pretenſion,
I find I'm unworthy of ſuch condeſcenſion,
And muſt, with regret, the high honour reſign,
Which I once vainly thought might with juſtice be
    mine.

SIR NICHOLAS.

Hey-day ! what does all this formality mean ?
Why, Dick ! has the Devil poſſeſs'd you with ſpleen ?
Or has love made your mind thus with diffidence ſore ?
Falſe modeſty ne'er was your foible before.

VOL. V.   R   You

You think you're unworthy !—the thought is fo new,
That I hardly can tell what to fay or to do.
If you love the good girl full as much as you faid,
I think you have very juft claims to her bed ;
But if your mind's chang'd, and you feel your love lighter,
'Tis better to fay fo, than marry and flight her :
And if this be the cafe, Sir, you have your releafe ;
For altho' I am eager to marry my Niece,
Tho' I'm partial to you, yet I beg you to note,
That I don't want to cram her down any man's throat.

DECISIVE.

I'm truly convinc'd of the Lady's perfection,
And 'twould pleafe me, dear Sir, to preferve the con-
   nection,
Tho' now, by particular reafons, I'm led
To revifit the Continent once ere I wed.
In the time of my abfence I can't be exact ;
But in what form you pleafe I will freely contract,
In the courfe of two years to receive as my Wife—

SIR NICHOLAS.

Do you mean to infult me, you puppy ? Od's-life !
Ere I'd tie my dear girl to fo filly a fop
For life, I'd condemn her to trundle a mop.

And

And let me advife you, young man, for the future,
To know your own mind ere you go as a fuitor.

DECISIVE.

I perceive, Sir, my prefence grows irkfome to you,
And you'll therefore allow me to bid you adieu.

SIR NICHOLAS.

Your departure, indeed, I don't wifh to reftrain,
And have little concern when I fee you again.

[*Exit* Decifive.

SIR NICHOLAS *alone.*

What can make this pert puppy recede from his fuit?
My fair Coufin and he have fcarce had a difpute;
She would hardly affront him on purpofe to vex me!—
Here fhe comes to explain all the points that perlex me.

Enter Mrs. Felix.

Well, Coufin, my fcheme, for a wedding's fufpended,
The Beaux are both gone, and their courtfhip is ended;
With an air fo myfterious Decifive withdraws,
I a little fufpect you're concern'd as the caufe:
Confefs, have you had any words with this Youth?

MRS. FELIX.

Not I, my dear Sir, on my honour and truth.
But I'm ready to own, that the news you impart
With furprize and with pleafure enlivens my heart.

R 2   I think

I think your fweet Niece has a lucky efcape :
I would almoft as foon fee her marry an ape
As her union with one of thefe coxcombs behold;
The Bard is too warm, and the Critic too cold.

SIR NICHOLAS.

I find that they are not fuch lads as I thought 'em;
The world all the worft of its fafhions has taught 'em :
And the world is indeed at a very fine pafs,
When fuch puppies infult fo attractive a lafs.
Young fellows of fortune now think it hard duty
To pay a chafte homage to Virtue and Beauty.
But I'll leave thefe pert fops to their own vile caprice,
And foon find a much fitter match for my Niece.
Other orders of men for a hufband I'll fearch,
And I think I can fettle my girl in the Church.

MRS. FELIX.

Lord, Coufin! I thought you detefted the Cloth!

SIR NICHOLAS.

Our Rector, I own, often kindles my wrath;
But all Parfons are not like my neighbour, old Squabble,
Who has learnt from his geefe both to hifs and to gobble.
We have in our neighbourhood three young Divines,
And each, I believe, to Selina inclines,

Our

Our Bishop's smart nephew deserves a sweet wench,
He himself in due time may be rais'd to the Bench;
With him I should like very well to unite her;
And if he hereafter should rise to the Mitre,
Then perhaps we together may bring to perfection
A much-wanted plan for the Church's correction.

MRS. FELIX.

A very fine scheme, which you'll manage, no doubt!

SIR NICHOLAS.

More wonderful things I have known brought about;
And tho' my first plan, as you see, has miscarried,
I'm resolv'd that my Niece shall be speedily married.
I'll unite the good girl to a Priest, if I'm able;
For the young Olive Branch never fails at his table.
There is one I prefer—but to leave the girl free,
I allow her to make a fair choice of the three:
I shall therefore invite the whole group to the hall,
And I'll now go and make her write cards to them all.

[*Exit.*

MRS. FELIX *alone.*

What a wonderful creature is this worthy Knight!
To make others happy is all his delight!
Yet, misled by some wild philanthropic illusion,
He's for ever involv'd in odd scenes of confusion.

R 3   'Tis

'Tis well that our Critic has made his laſt bow,
I rejoice he's remov'd, and I long to know how.

Enter Morley.

M o r l e y.

Thank my ſtars, my dear Ma'am, I've diſpatch'd your
    commiſſion ;
Your ſweet friend is, I hope, in a tranquil condi-
    tion :
From her two irkſome lovers ſhe now is reliev'd.

M r s. F e l i x.

And I'm dying to know how all this was atchiev'd.
Come tell me, good creature, how could you ef-
    fect it ?

M o r l e y.

By a project ſo ſimple you'd never ſuſpect it :
I have baniſh'd both ſwains, by declaring a wife
Would rob one of glory, and t'other of life.
I perſuaded the Bard his poetical fame
Could never exiſt with a conjugal flame :
Hence he grew with your charms ſo licentiouſly free,
But forgive me this ill, which I could not foreſee.
Deciſive, more wiſely, abandons the Fair
To make his own lungs his particular care.

M r s.

MRS. FELIX.

What ! on fuch points as thefe have they taken your
    word ?

MORLEY.

Dear Madam ! mankind credit things moft abfurd,
When they come from the mouth of a medical man ;
Hence Mountebanks never want fkill to trepan.
The extent of our empire indeed there's no feeing,
When we act on the fears of a true felfifh being.

MRS. FELIX.

How fimple foever the means you've employ'd,
You have remedy'd ills by which we were annoy'd.
Having thus clear'd the fcene from each troublefome
    lover,
Can you not for the nymph a fit hufband difcover ?
You fee how fhe's preft by her Uncle to wed,
Who ne'er quits a fcheme he once takes in his head.——
Suppofe her kind fancy fhould lean towards you,
Is your heart quite as free as I'm fure 'twould be true ?
Is it not pre-engag'd ?

MORLEY.

        As in mirth's fportive fally
It pleafes you thus a poor pilgrim to rally,

        Your

Your good-nature, I know, will forgive me if I
To your pleafantry make a too ferious reply.
'Tis my maxim to fpeak, whatfoe'er be the theme,
With a heart undifguis'd, to the friends I efteem : ·
Had I all India's wealth, 'twould be my inclination
To offer it all to your lovely relation.
But fuppofing it poffible you could be willing
To unite her with one who is fcarce worth a fhilling ;
Believe me, dear Madam, my pride is too great
To wifh her to ftoop to my humble eftate.

Mrs. Felix.

Such pride, tho' it refts upon no ftrong foundation,
Is noble I own, and deferves admiration.
I call it ill-founded, becaufe, in my mind,
If there's fortune enough for a couple when join'd,
If talents and worth are by each duly fhar'd,
If in all other points they are equally pair'd, ·
And mutual regard mutual merit enhances,
It fignifies not which fupply'd their finances.

Morley.

Your pardon—how often, when fortune's unequal,
Gay weddings produce a moft turbulent fequel ?
But could I once hope your fweet Coufin to gain,
How many things are there fuch hopes to reftrain ?

Suppofe

Suppofe your dear Colonel, my moft noble friend,

Whom fuccefs to your arms may more fpeedily fend!

Suppofe, having clos'd the bright work he has plan'd,

His return from the Eaft he fhould haften by land;

Suppofe him arriv'd, with what face could I meet

The man whom my heart fhould exultingly greet,

If he found me attempting, in fpite of my ftation.

To wed, tho' a beggar, your wealthy relation?

M R s. F E L I x.

From thefe words, my dear friend, which I almoft
    adore,

And a few flighter hints that efcap'd you before,

I have caught a quick hope, which is fraught with
    delight,

That I foon fhall be bleft with my Felix's fight:

I begin to fufpect he's in England already;

I perceive that you can't keep your countenance fteady.

With his ufual attention his love has reflected

How my poor foolifh nerves by furprize are affected;

And, left they fhould fail me beyond all revival,

Has fent you to prepare for his wifh'd-for arrival.

Am I right in my guefs? Is he not very near?

Could I truft my own heart, I fhould think Felix here.

C o l o n e l.

Colonel Felix, *entering.*

Sweet foreboder, behold him reſtor'd to your arms.

Mrs. Felix.

O my Felix! this tranſport o'erpays all alarms,
Thus to ſee thee reſtor'd, and ennobled with fame!
In what words ſhall affection thy welcome proclaim?

Colonel.

My Love! my beſt Treaſure! than glory more dear!
The bliſs of this meeting, which ſhines in thy tear,
That we owe to this friend let us never forget.

Morley.

My ſhare in your tranſport o'erpays all the debt—
But, Colonel, your fondneſs has travell'd full ſpeed,
And has not allow'd me the time you agreed.

Colonel.

I meant not, indeed, to have join'd you to-day,
But I found love forbade my intended delay.

Morley.

Well, my duty is done, now you happily meet;
Heaven bleſs you together—

Mrs. Felix.

Stay, ſtay, I entreat;
You muſt not go yet; and before you depart
I will open to Felix the ſcheme of my heart.

B   SELINA.

SELINA *(behind the scene.)*

Indeed, Sir, I never can write such a card.

SIR NICHOLAS *(behind the scene.)*

Then you'll forfeit at once my paternal regard!

COLONEL.

Hey-day! in the house I much fear something's wrong,
As Sir Nicholas talks in a language so strong.

MRS. FELIX.

Does he know you are here?

COLONEL.

No, my dear, I think not,
Unless he the tidings from Jenny has got;
She alone saw me come, and without much ado
Most kindly directed me where to find you.

MRS. FELIX.

They are coming this way—let's withdraw all together,
And contrive how to turn this loud storm to fair
    weather.   *[Exeunt.*

Enter Sir Nicholas *and* Selina.

SIR NICHOLAS.

I insist on your writing such cards to them all!

SELINA.

Dear Uncle, I beg you'll this order recall.

                      You

You know your commands I much wish to obey;
But reflect on this matter what people will say:
You're so eager to marry your Niece, they will swear
That you hawk her about just like goods at a fair.

SIR NICHOLAS.

Well, my dear, let'em say so, and I'll say so too,
For your simile proves what a guardian should do.
He who wants to dispose of a tender young maid,
May take a good hint from the gingerbread trade:
If he has any sense, 'twill be ever his plan
To part with soft pastry as soon as he can;
For egad an old maid is like old harden'd paste,
You may cry it about, but nobody will taste.
Come, do as I bid you, and take up your pen.

SELINA.

Lord, Sir ! it will seem very odd to these men;
You will make me appear in a horrible light;
I vow my hand shakes so, I never can write.
Excuse me, dear Sir, from this business, pray do,
And let me live single for ever with you.

SIR NICHOLAS,

All business where woman's concern'd, I believe,
Must partake of the curse from our grandmother Eve.

All

All her daughters the steps of their parent have follow'd!

Contradiction, the core of the apple she swallow'd,

In their veins still fermenting new ills can produce,

And all their blood seems coloquintida juice.——

You froward cross baggage! your word should I take,

And bid you live single five years for my sake,

Of the barbarous Uncle you'd quickly complain,

Who from nature's just right a young girl wou'd
 restrain!

SELINA.

Indeed, Sir, I should not.

SIR NICHOLAS.

      I tell you you wou'd.

From perverseness alone you oppose your own good.

'Tis only to thwart me, because I desire

To see you well settled before I expire,

That you now, with your soft hypocritcal carriage,

Affect to have no inclination to marriage.

But you'll never contrive, tho' your tongue may be
 nimble,

To convince me your heart is as cold as your thimble.

I know of what stuff froward damsels are made;

The guardian must force you, who cannot persuade.

        That

That you'll like a good hufband, I never can doubt;
And married you fhall be before the month's out,
Or at leaft your kind Uncle no more you fhall teaze,
But may e'en go to Rome and turn nun if you pleafe.

SELINA (afide:)

I have loft all the love he has fhewn me for year);
If I ftrive to reply I fhall burft into tears.

SIR NICHOLAS.

Come, anfwer me, Mifs! will you fcribble or not?

Enter the Colonel, Mrs. Felix, and Morley.

COLONEL.

My worthy old friend, what can make you fo hot?

SIR NICHOLAS.

Ha, Colonel!—you find me a little concern'd—
But I'm heartily glad you are fafely return'd.
Your arrival indeed is a welcome furprize,
Tho' before you your fame a bright harbinger flies;
We have heard your fuccefs, and we all triumph in it.

COLONEL.

I truft I am come in a fortunate minute
To make all your prefent embarraffment ceafe,
For I bring a young hufband, my friend, for your
     Niece.

SIR

SIR NICHOLAS.

Egad, that's well faid; and I'm fure it's well meant;
And if he's like you he fhall have my confent.

COLONEL.

He has many more virtues, and juft as much wealth,
And from India brings home both his morals and health.
Here, my friend, is the man.—As I owe him my life,
I wifh to prefent him fo lovely a wife;
Half my fortune is his—here I freely declare it,
And have only to hope that Selina may fhare it.
I've regarded her long as a child of my own;
Nor can my affection more truly be fhown,
Than by wifhing to place the dear girl in the arms
Of the friend whofe rare virtues are worthy her charms.

MORLEY.

Dear generous Felix, I'm quite overcome,
Thy bounty is fuch, it ftrikes gratitude dumb!

COLONEL.

This was ever, my friend, my moft fettled intention,
Though my very juft purpofe I chofe not to mention,
From the hope I fhould find, what I gladly embrace,
A moment from which it may borrow fome grace,
When my gift its plain value may rife far above,
By the aid it affords to the wifhes of love;

And

And I own, as a prophet I'm proud of my art,
Now I fee the effects of her charms on your heart.

MORLEY.

O Felix! can I thus deprive thy free fpirit
Of wealth, the reward of heroical merit ?
Can I the victorious Commander defpoil
Of what he has purchas'd with danger and toil ?
Should love and delight on thy prefent attend,
I could never be happy in robbing a friend.
No, I ftill muft decline—

SIR NICHOLAS.

My dear boy, fay no more;
You're the match that I never could meet with before.
I have long fought in vain for an heir to my mind,
But all my foul wifh'd, in your fpirit I find.
You fhall *not* rob your friend of a fingle * Gold Moor,
He can raife heirs enough to inherit his ftore:
To fuch men as himfelf let him hafte to give birth,
And with twenty young Felix's garnifh the earth.
How trifling foever your fortune may be;
From the Colonel's efteem, and the virtues I fee,
I think you as noble a match for my Niece,
As I could, had you brought home a new golden fleece:

* An Indian Coin.

I have money enough, if you're rich in affection.—
As I always have talk'd of an equal connection,
My neighbours, perhaps, may suppose my fight dim,
Or mock my wife choice as a generous whim :
Let them study with zeal, which I hope may succeed,
Of their horses and dogs to improve the best breed ;
A study more noble engrosses my mind,
To preserve the first points in the breed of mankind :
On the heart and the soul, as the first points, I dwell,
In these, my dear Children, you match mighty well ;
And I think human nature in debt to my care,
For uniting two mortals who happily pair.

COLONEL.

Your hand, my dear Knight, it is gloriously said !

SIR NICHOLAS.

By Juno, we'll put the young Couple to bed !
We'll have no dull delays.—

MRS. FELIX.

Now what say you, my dear
Are these orders for marriage too quick and severe ?

MORLEY.

My amazement and gratitude both are extreme,
But my voice seems opprest in a heavenly dream ;

Though your kindnefs is greater than language can paint,
I beg this fair hand may be free from conftraint.

SIR NICHOLAS.

From conftraint !—Gad, if now fhe affects to demur,
I can tell her my wrath fhe will fo far incur,
She fhall go to a convent for life, or at leaft
Be fent as a venture herfelf to the Eaft.

SELINA.

My Uncle I long have obey'd, and at prefent
I cannot complain his commands are unpleafant :
Nay more ; could he place all mankind in my view,
And bid me chufe from them, my choice would be you.

MORLEY.

To this dear declaration my life muft reply,
All words are too weak——

SIR NICHOLAS.

The whole earth I defy,
To fhew me a fcene more delightful than this ;
Dear honeft frank Girl, come and give me a kifs ;
Thou'rt the creature of Nature much more than of Art,
And I own thee again as the Child of my heart.

JONATHAN, *entering and fpeaking to the* Colonel.

There are two chefts for you, Sir, juft come to the hall.

COLONEL.

A few Indian things for the Ladies—that's all.

Pray, Jonathan, pay thofe who brought them with this. *(giving money.)*

MORLEY.

My brave lad muft fhare in our general blifs.

Here Jonathan, if you're to marriage inclin'd,

And can luckily meet with a girl to your mind,

You may marry and fettle, as foon as you pleafe;

The Colonel has taken good care of your eafe.

JONATHAN.

God blefs him, whate'er he is pleas'd to beftow!

I think I have found a kind fweetheart below.

MRS. FELIX.

He has made choice of Jenny;—and I will provide

A fortune, my Friend, for your good-humour'd Bride.

SIR NICHOLAS.

Egad, they fhall have my new farm on the hill,

And raife young recruits there as faft as they will.

JONATHAN.

Heaven profper you all! I will pray for you ever,

And to ferve my King ftill, as I can, I'll endeavour.

[*Exit.*

SIR NICHOLAS.

Well faid, honeft Soldier;—we'll have no delay,

Go and tell the old Parfon to keep in the way.

8   COLONEL.

COLONEL.

Come with me, fair Cousin, examine my chests;
I long to present you a few bridal vests.

MRS. FELIX, *to* Morley.

As we view with delight the events of to-day,
A fair lesson, my Friend, in your fate we survey;
While, from love to an aged fond parent, with speed
From wealth's open road you most kindly recede,
Heaven sends you that fortune you nobly have flighed,
And your warm filial piety here is requited;
This bright moral truth by your lot is exprest,
They who seek others' bliss, are by Providence blest.

SIR NICHOLAS, *to* Morley.

Here, my worthy young Friend, take and cherish this
          Fair,
And, trust me, you'll find her deserving your care;
For although of her sex she may have a small spice,
She'll please you ten times where she vexes you twice;
And happy the man, in this skirmishing life,
Who is able to say half so much of his Wife.

END OF THE FIFTH VOLUME.

www.ingramcontent.com/pod-product-compliance
Lightning Source LLC
Chambersburg PA
CBHW030643030726
47497CB00006B/1929